Sinead King lives in a leafy English village. Having always been a keen reader, with an innate passion for writing, Sinead decided that it was time to fulfil a lifelong ambition and to produce her first book. She found the writing process to be highly rewarding.

Sinead is currently busy working on her second book.

For James – we got there in the end.

Sinead King

CONDEMNED

AUSTIN MACAULEY PUBLISHERS™
LONDON * CAMBRIDGE * NEW YORK * SHARJAH

A CIP catalogue record for this title is available from the British Library.

ISBN 9781398491847 (Paperback)
ISBN 9781398491854 (ePub e-book)

www.austinmacauley.com

First Published 2023
Austin Macauley Publishers Ltd®
1 Canada Square
Canary Wharf
London
E14 5AA

2024/02/14

I would love to thank all of the incredible people in my life for their support and encouragement. I am so proud to have such a wonderful Mum and such amazing friends – you all mean the world to me.

I would love to offer my profound thanks to the Austin Macauley Publishers team for all of their assistance.

Now

It's funny how we're all rather guilty of trundling through life; failing to stop; failing to see the little things, that so often we realise were the *big* things at a later date. I have lived in the same house for twenty-four years and I never noticed how many photographs were on my fireplace. Not until now, anyway. There was a photograph of my wedding day – I'm always so shocked by how *young* I look. You wouldn't have thought I was twenty-one in that photo, not a chance. I look so baby-faced; my hair falling right down to my waist (as that was when I was at an age when it was still quite passable to resemble Goldilocks and to not look ridiculous, into the bargain). My hair was blowing in the breeze in the photo and I was extremely conscious that my heels were starting to sink into the grass at an alarmingly fast rate, but I remember feeling as though I could burst with joy at that moment. I can remember holding on to Tom, who looked at me, in such a way that my heart skipped a beat. I first clapped eyes on him at seventeen and I can vividly recall myself thinking: *If fairy tales truly do exist and I really am supposed to end up with Prince Charming, please let it be that I end up marrying Tom Wright.*

I remember him sauntering up to me for the first time; a gleam in his eye; a swing in his step. As cheesy as it sounds, he had me at hello.

I remembered how he'd made every twee, excruciating *relationship* I had had, up until this point seem utterly irrelevant. When he'd proposed to me the day before my twenty-first birthday, I didn't hesitate in jumping at the chance. Much to my parents' dismay. With Tom being seven years older than me, I had foregone university as I couldn't bear the thought of being separated from him for months on end. I had known at the time that this decision had devastated my parents. They whined that I showed such potential; such *promise* and wheedled with me to reconsider. After a lifetime of having always been the mild-mannered; studious daughter that didn't constantly bring embarrassment and trouble to their doorstep (they needed at least one dependable bet, with Polly having always been such an egotistical magnet for spectacles and spite), I, for the first time in history, did not waver. My parents and I were embroiled in an unmovable deadlock. They were beside themselves at the fact that as far as they could see, I was deftly throwing away my education and future for a fly-by-knight. I vividly recalled my mother weeping that I would understand where she was coming from when I had children myself one day, she perceived it that my late teens and early twenties were for going out and enjoying myself; having no ties and attaining a degree that would serve me superbly in the future. My mother had always been wistful about university. She'd have ached to have had the opportunity to study for a degree, but she had always argued that life simply got in the way. That's why she was so disappointed that I was so keen to settle down with Tom so young. She saw it that I had the world at my feet and that I was discarding making something of my life because I was so desperate to become a wife. I always remembered her snippily making the assumption that I'd probably wind up becoming a very bitter little old wife by the age of thirty, because, in all likelihood, I'd be laden with three kids, trying to get a yoghurt stain off my blouse, wondering if this was simply *it*.

I remember my mother frequently said, "You're only a baby. I know you think that you're sussed and you always think that you know everything there is to know when you're young, but you've got to spend these years focusing on yourself. You won't get the time back again, darling."

I remembered it was one of the only times that I actually blatantly went against my mum's wishes. I was adamant that I was ditching higher education, in favour of settling down with Tom. There would be periodic blow-ups about this decision over the next few years that followed, prior to the wedding. I think it would be impossible to forget my father saying thickly to me as he fought back tears the evening before my wedding, "We just feel like we're losing you, Susanna. Your life has barely begun and already you're racing down the aisle. We're just terrified that you're going to wake up one day and be so terribly sad, that you never really had the opportunity to get out there and to live."

It's ironic really that my parents were both so fixated on me becoming an unhappy little wife, chained to Tom's side for the rest of my life. They failed to see that he made me feel more alive than anyone; they struggled to understand that I had never been particularly career orientated. Sure, I'd kept my head down at school, did well in my exams, but that didn't mean in the same breath that I had to go off and become a CEO; spend my twenties living the *Young*

Professional High Life, and then end up marrying in my thirties before having two children (a boy and a girl as then they'd have a grandson and a granddaughter, one of each that they could boast about at their tennis club. I think even then my parents perceived me as the horse to back on the grandchildren's front, as Polly had always been known to spend her Saturday mornings in last night's, *going out*, clothes and stilettos after having met a very unsuitable stranger the evening before, as opposed to feeding the ducks whilst wearing shabby trainers, like me.) I can recall, my parents approaching me on my wedding day after all of the photos had been taken and how they said in a low, holy whisper as though they were talking in church, "We are truly glad that you're happy, Suzie. But it's just not what we would have planned for you."

I wouldn't have planned on losing Tom four years after marrying him. He died after an excruciating battle with acute myeloid leukaemia. Terribly shocking; terribly upsetting. Particularly upsetting, given that the day Tom was diagnosed with the godforsaken illness, I already had a definable curve forming beneath my jumper, reminding me that one way or another, whatever happened, I was going to have to keep it together. It wasn't just me anymore, there was James to look after now.

Tom died a fortnight before James was born. We'd known beforehand that we were having a boy and he had been absolutely over the moon. I'd simply assumed that he would want a Tom Junior and was more than happy to go along with this, but he had surprised me when he said suddenly that he was desperate for him to be called James. A strong name for his strong boy. It seemed perfect. It's strange that for so long, that had been the hardest fortnight spell of my life, knowing that I was about to have a baby, two weeks after the love of my life had died. My friends were always stunned at how I just *carried on*, my mantra was simple: *Because I had to*. James was dependent upon me.

I remembered holding him as a newborn – wide-eyed and perfect, with that air of wisdom and knowledge that all babies are born with. I remember looking at him; my heart feeling like it was going to burst out of my chest with love. I don't think I'll ever be able to forget my mum's anguished sobs, as she regarded me cuddling him close, utterly oblivious to the madness of the world around me, as suddenly, I had my baby and he made everything make sense and seem worthwhile. I'll always remember the desperation in my mum's voice as she said, "Oh Susanna, however are you going to manage?"

And it's strange because I can't describe how or why but I just remember staring down at James and thinking, *It's going to be okay as long as I've got you. We're in this together. We've got this.*

It's so surreal to think that for such a long time, the most painful thing that ever happened to me was losing Tom. I liked having his photos around the house for years, but at one point, I remember becoming aware of the fact that it was becoming somewhat shrine-like. James was toddling about at that stage and I remember feeling conscious that I didn't want him to feel as though he was exploring a permanent vigil for his father. I never wanted him to grow up, feeling as though he was in his shadow. The only photo displayed of Tom now is the one on our wedding day. I glanced at it. It was all so *cruel.*

I turned away from the photos on the fireplace, which was laden with all of these pointless photos, all these bland ones of me with my arms around my parents; a daft one of my closest friend, Karen and I looking like a pair of prats in line-dancing costumes and really ironically, one of Polly and I as teenagers, pouting at the camera with our arms linked, despite the fact that we'd have probably have had a huge spat two minutes before the camera flashed. Spun around away from the fireplace, I looked at all of the photos on the floor, spread out across every inch of the carpet. There was a sea of smiling Jamies from every single angle with which I looked at. I looked at James, a curly haired baby; chubby and cuddly, the type of infant that old ladies cross over the road to coo and ooh over. There he was again, as a cheeky toddler this time, with chocolate smeared around his mouth, utterly adorable. I saw him as a grinning seven-year-old, clad in an alligator costume for *World Book Day*; larking around sun-kissed on the beach in Alicante; dancing around with Mr Jones; our dear old dog that he thought the world of. I felt momentarily faint.

I stumbled to the sofa. There were more photos here, piles and piles of them. There was James on his 21st, only a few weeks previously. Ever the joker, he was dressed as Superman. Max, his best friend, stood to his left and laughed heartily at some witty remark Jamie had just made. Meanwhile his girlfriend Rachel gazing up at him adoringly from his right, as he wound his arm round her lovingly. There were some photos of James with Adam, but I didn't like to look at those so I quickly put them to one side, faced down.

Polly suddenly came into the room. She looked momentarily anxious but she rapidly tried to disguise her fear, by purposefully tucking her hair behind her ears and ostentatiously clearing her throat. "Susanna, the tea's ready. Come to the table and I'll get you something to eat as well. How about some toast?"

I'd stopped listening. Honestly, I couldn't take her seriously. Polly; Polly put the kettle on. Polly, the lush. Polly, the man-stealer. Polly, the joke. The sight of her trying to be all mumsy as she bustles about with tea is almost laughable. We both know that she'd give anything to be anywhere else.

Polly looked helpless. She was all set to plead.

"Susanna, come to the table. You can't just stay there all day. Come on, you don't want your Adam seeing you like this, do you?"

She sighed, before muttering despairingly, "Again."

Polly approached me; she was practically on her knees, talking in a faux-upbeat tone. The sort of tone you would use when speaking to a small child.

"Can you imagine how happy Adam would be if he came in and saw you sitting up at the table, looking after yourself for once? You must be starving."

She was practically pulling at her hair now.

"You must be."

It's strange her even being here; there's something peculiar about her even being in my living room. She seemed to be thinking the same. Polly's not really used to having to care for people. She's selfish to the core; unless something or someone benefits her, she doesn't want to know. However, she's all too aware that the neighbours will start talking if she's not seen to be making her presence felt at a time like this. It would be callous; uncaring; utterly outrageous, if she didn't fuss around here all the time, pouring cups of tea and making scones and breathing down my neck, twenty-four hours a day. It's incredible to me that she didn't appear to have cottoned on to the fact that I am fully aware of her motives, it's excruciating for her to have to play, *House* with me, of all people, who she's never exactly seen eye to eye with. I wished she'd just *go*; beetle off to her own place, but she wasn't going to do that anytime soon. People would notice; they'd find it noteworthy for all of the wrong reasons. Polly is too concerned with public perception to be a person that lives her life completely authentically.

Polly had started to become flustered at this point.

"Susanna, I really didn't want to tell you this because God knows you've got enough on your plate. But Adam, he's truly heartbroken, plain and simple. He drifts around looking like a little ghost half the time. I try my utmost with him, I really do, but an aunt is a far cry from a mother. He needs you to look after him; you need to look after each-other."

She'd obviously read some sort of self-help book. Polly is always reading self-help books. Usually, she's seemingly content with being a one-woman disaster zone but there are sometimes occasions where she seems to possess a seed of self-awareness and grows conscious of the fact that she is a mess. She buys a handful from Waterstones every couple of Saturdays and vows that that day, yes, that day, was going to be when she began the rest of her life. She'd be a vegan for a day or so as she had read continually that this healed your mind; she'd vow to ditch the daily glass of wine; omit to pop into the bakery for her Vanilla Crème Horn every morning before work. She'd drop a dress size or so and become a worldly and wise goddess in next to no time. Usually after two days; she'd collapse on to the sofa and devour two takeaways; a bottle of wine and a box of blueberry muffins, as she'd insist that life is fundamentally too short for her to deprive herself.

I looked away from Polly, her attention-seeking neediness was really starting to grate on me. I stared at a photograph of James instead; he was only about four and was smiling widely, as he was given a piggyback by me. I felt myself welling up.

"I love my son so much," I said, my words barely audible.

Polly clearly had the hearing of a bat. She rubbed her face wearily.

"I know. I know how much you love Adam. I just know that because of everything…"

She looked temporarily tearful, but she quickly poised herself. It's interesting that seeing her wobbly evokes no emotion for me whatsoever.

Polly swallowed; she was building up to something.

"I just think that with everything that's happened, and let's face it, words can never quite explain just how horrendous this has all been that Adam can sometimes feel a bit invisible."

Here she goes again. I am sick and tired of hearing her bleat on about him.

"I adore my son," I said, my chin jutting.

"My Jamie."

At this, I happened to glance down at the wastepaper bin. It was heaving, it was full to the brim with cards. With sympathy cards. One of the messages was visible, "We are so sorry for your loss Susanna and Adam. There are no words to express how very sad we are. Jamie was a wonderful young man who brought so much happiness and hope to anyone that encountered him. Our hearts hurt for you. We are always here at the end of the phone if either of you wishes to talk. Love Karen, Geoff and family xx."

I looked at a photograph of Jamie and I, it was recent; only taken a few weeks ago. On the eve of his 21st. We were sitting in this exact spot; he had his arm around my shoulders; we were both beaming. I felt briefly winded as though someone had knocked the breath out of my body.

I wasn't aware of the tears rolling down my face until Polly patted my hand, as she got to her feet. "I'll bring the tea in here, eh?" she said, the words escaping her in a choked whisper.

Polly left the room. I stayed marooned on the sofa; motionless; lifeless. I heard some boys from across the road career up and down on bicycles; laughing exuberantly.

"Come on, James!" called a boy.

I looked at my James. A silent tear rolled down my cheek.

Then

"Right, that's dinner all good to go now!" I called as I headed out of the kitchen, making for the dining table. The huge lasagne dish I held was steaming hot. I silently debated as to whether I'd perhaps gone slightly over the top on the cheese front, but I decided that it was probably best to have too much as opposed to too little, after all.

Jamie was sitting at the table, trying patiently to engage with Adam. As per usual, he uttered a grunt. Trying to converse with him is like attempting to get blood out of a stone. I knew that Jamie would probably perceive having a root canal as being the better alternative to speaking with him, but he was doing his utmost to spark some conversation. That's Jamie all over, nobody could ever accuse him of not being inclusive. As far as I'm concerned, a saint would be pushed to the brink if they had to have a meal with Adam, but Jamie preserved, with his usual sunny optimism. I wished so badly that I could take a leaf out of his book; know somehow what to say to Adam. I felt his stare on me, as I bustled to the table, laden with lasagne. There was something so penetrating; so alarming about his stare. He rarely made eye contact. He usually only opted to look at me straight on when I was distracted and not glancing in his direction. I felt my hands shake slightly under his scrutiny. I saw the flash of his smirk; taunting and smug, from the corner of my eye. Instinctively, I felt a queasy sense of sickly anticipation. I knew that smirk all too well.

I tried to mask my anxiety and started to cheerfully witter on about having made enough food to cater for a small village; so I really hoped that they were both famished. Jamie laughed and instantly, I felt a warm surge of ease. He made things better, just by being him. It wasn't just Adam and I at this table. Nothing bad was going to happen. That's what I had to remember.

"You know me, I'm always hungry! Bottomless pit, my stomach!" he said jovially.

I registered Jamie: despite towering over me at a whopping six feet three and resembling a tree trunk in terms of stature and build, he never exuded a threatening effect, the way you would have assumed someone of his size would have done. He was someone that simply made you feel safe; he was strong, capable, and measured. Standing with him by your side, always felt like standing with an army. It was rare to meet people like that; people that could alleviate all of your anxieties, even just for a moment, with a simple grin, or a waggle of his eyebrows or a hand on your shoulder. I knew people spoke about those souls that really do just light up whatever room they go into, but Jamie always seemed to take that up a dial or so. He wouldn't just light up a room, he'd dance around all of those people who were in the room too; his brightness and zeal so infectious, that you would feel for just a split second, it was a trait that you could encapsulate too. It's a skill to be a people-person; most people struggle to interact these days. They communicate through monosyllabic mumbles and grunts; barely able to hold down a five-minute conversation. That's sort of the magic about Jamie, he doesn't just lift people's spirits and improve the mood. He brings the best out of them; he seems to have this metaphorical key that can access the very best parts of people that no one else could identify them with. I'd say that Jamie is most certainly, a *glass-half-full* kind of guy, but I know he'd erupt with laughter if I was to say that to him. He'd correct me anyway and say I was missing the point with that whole analogy: after all, glasses are refillable!

The personification of a glass drained of all drops of drink whatsoever would be Adam. He sat beside Jamie; slouching to such an extent that his chin was practically resting on his chest. I'd worried about his posture when he was small; fretted about him having scoliosis. That wasn't the case. He could uncurl himself when he wanted to. He just chose not to, most of the time. He always resembled a snake lurking in the long grass; wishing to lull you into a false sense of security by making you think he was smaller and more defenceless than he was. But then, just when you'd assume that it was all in your head and you were merely a paranoid wreck; he'd turn at the drop of a hat and hiss; exposing the foul, forked tongue that lay inside his mouth. I eyed him briefly as I started serving up great hearty portions of lasagne. He looked removed, yet resentful. I felt sick. I turned to Jamie.

"Right, J, I've given you a good 5/8. I know that you've always been able to eat for England! Adam, how much would you like, love?"

The strain is unbearable. He can go weeks without uttering a single word to me. He likes to punish me, more often than not, for no reason at all. He enjoys watching me begging; grovelling. When he does eventually speak to me, he'll usually malevolently whisper something vengeful and vindictive whenever Jamie is out of earshot, or he'll attempt to gaslight me into believing that there had never been any silent treatment; there was no issue. He'd dub me as sensitive; an overthinker. An imagination too active for my own good. It was easier to believe that, years ago. I wanted to believe it. It seemed the better option, the superior alternative to facing the truth. Jamie looked at Adam; he's irked, the silence has gone on too long. Adam shifts in his seat, he's aware that Jamie may start to put the thumbscrews on at any minute.

"I'll just have a bit," Adam said flatly. I found myself letting out a small breath that I didn't realise I'd been holding. He was speaking and he didn't sound like he was gearing up to be acidic. Perhaps I had simply got the wrong end of the stick earlier? Maybe he wasn't on the attack. I found myself relaxing slightly. Jamie grinned.

"I wouldn't have thought old Ads would need much dinner. After all, you had a colossal pizza only about an hour ago!"

He tucks into his own dinner, suddenly ravenous.

"So, go on then Romeo. I want all the juicy details as to how your hot pizza date with Kayleigh Winters went?"

Jamie patted Adam on the arm encouragingly.

"I can't believe you weren't even going to ask her out until I set you straight."

This was a perfect way to try and talk to Adam. I took a breath inwardly. It was difficult to know what to say to him exactly as the most throwaway remarks could trigger him, but I thought that this was a relatively safe conversational topic. I decided to go for it.

"Why weren't you going to ask her out before, love?" I animatedly quizzed Adam.

He stared at me; his demeanour was subdued yet contrastingly stealthy.

"I just wasn't."

I felt fleetingly dissatisfied before I felt a hand give my own a quick squeeze beneath the table. *Jamie's*. I felt consoled.

Jamie grinned broadly.

"Unfortunately, our Ads failed to see what a catch he is, Mum. He had cold feet before, thinking that pretty little Kayleigh wouldn't give him a second look.

What a load of bollocks that turned out to be. She bit your hand off when you asked her, didn't she, Adam?"

Adam was unreadable beside him. I was too quick to dive in with reassurance, that was a big mistake.

"Honestly, Adam, any girl should consider herself lucky to be on your arm. You're such a great guy."

Adam looked me straight in the eye. There was something dangerous about his directness.

"Am I? Why's that?" he demanded.

I was stumped. It was a seemingly simple question, but I really had no idea as to how I should answer. I felt like my brain was filled with fog. I tried to think of something glib; generic that I could say, but I seemed to have lost the ability to think. I felt paralysed. Jamie rescued me.

Intervening smoothly, he said, "You're interesting. You've got the whole elusive enigma vibe that the girls go wild for. Your personal hygiene is good, I mean, you actually wear clean socks every day. Trust me, I think if I wore clean socks every day, Rachel would think I was the next best thing since sliced bread. Or Nutella. I mean Christ, it doesn't even bear thinking about a time when toast didn't have Nutella to join it."

He gave a pantomime shudder.

"Breakfast in the Middle Ages, it must have been horrific."

I laughed joyously. Evidently resentful of the happiness showcased before him, Adam interjected, his tone cool and atmosphere altering.

"The only reason Kayleigh Winters agreed to go out with me was because I'm the half-brother of Jamie Wright. Otherwise, she'd have said no to the nobody that is me in a flash."

Internally, I found myself groaning. Brilliant, Adam harping on about the whole, *We're only half-brothers,* saga again. For having only been intimate with two men in my life, I had had a child with both of them. When Jamie was nearly three, I'd met Dean, Adam's father. It was hardly the love-story of the century. He was bland, boring, unexciting. Everything Tom wasn't. He sloped around the house in shirts that smelt musty and he lacked oomph; charisma. Dean's get-up-and-go had got up and gone. At first, I'd been concerned that he may be depressed, but I soon discovered that he was just bone-idle. Naturally unmotivated and as messy as sin, I soon realised that I'd effectively moved a mid-thirties man-child into my home. I was all set to send Dean packing about six months after he had moved in with Jamie and I. Two blue lines on a pregnancy test changed that. I remembered the sinking feeling of knowing that I'd have to, "put up and shut up". I'd have to try and make things work with him, for the baby's sake at least. For Jamie's sake too. That was another thing – Dean was amazing with Jamie. They got on like a house on fire. He was so hands-on, so involved. I'd assumed that Dean would probably be one of those men that was a better father than a partner. He'd suggested we marry when I told him I was expecting Adam. I knew he didn't particularly want to; it was just the done thing. I made it clear that the only man I was going to have married in my life would be Tom. He seemed to get it; I don't recall him ever having really pressed it. But we never really talked much. In the days, our focus was entirely on Jamie. In the evenings, when he was in bed, we'd sit in front of the TV gormlessly, barely exchanging a word. We'd briefly talk about the weather now and again; decide upon who'd take Jamie into town to get him some new shoes; whose turn was it to go to the supermarket as we were out of butter and milk. His arm would always snake across my waist in bed on a Saturday night; as ingrained into our maddening routine as watching *EastEnders* in silence, evening after evening.

I'd simply assumed that because Dean had always been such a brilliant stepdad to Jamie, he'd be a good father to his own child too. However, Jamie and Adam were so *different*. Jamie was so personable, so adventure loving, and so buoyant. Whereas Adam had always been cold, hostile, and strange. Dean openly admitted to struggling to find a connection with him. I remembered telling my best friend Karen this at the time and her gasping that it was such an awful thing to say about your own baby. I went through the motions of nodding along with her, but privately, I knew what Dean meant. He just voiced aloud what I wasn't brave enough to admit. Dean wanted a mini-me and in many respects, he had that in Jamie. Dean was big and broad; Adam was small and scrawny. Dean was a geezer; Adam was an oddity. Dean simply assumed that Adam would be a younger version of Jamie, but the reality was, that couldn't be further from the truth. They were always chalk and cheese. Dean ended up walking out when Adam was six. He'd upgraded to a younger model; he wanted to rush off into the sunset with her. I can't recall feeling particularly crestfallen; Dean and I had an okay dynamic, but we were more like acquaintances in a house-share. We could make small talk as we both waited to use the kettle or waved goodbye to each other in the mornings, but I think we were both all too aware that we had co-existed for a long time. The only person really saddened by Dean's departure was Jamie. Dean still kept in contact with Jamie for a year or so after he left but he wasn't massively bothered about maintaining a relationship with Adam. The irony is that Dean's departure made very little difference to Adam's day-to-day life, but he harboured that feeling of rejection ever since. He felt discarded; demeaned. He didn't blame Dean. He blamed me.

Adam curled his lip.

"If I was an only child, Kayleigh would never have agreed to go out with me."

I snapped back into the situation.

Jamie rolled his eyes.

"For God's sake, you muppet, you need to stop bleating on about us being half-brothers. It does my head in, do you know that?"

He tried to lighten the mood.

"You just need to accept that Kayleigh clearly has hungry eyes…"

He launched into the *Dirty Dancing* song, prompting me to erupt. Even Adam couldn't resist smiling slightly.

Jamie ruffled Adam's hair.

"You just have to accept, you wally, that she's into you. You've got the heart of a really nice girl and it means you can finally have a bit of lurve in your life. And Christ knows that you need a bit of romance."

I tensed. I feared that Adam was going to interpret this as a thinly veiled dig. Adam really was a *very* late developer in that regard. Jamie was always a total hit with the girls; he had streams of moon-eyed girls drifting around after him all the time, desperate to be with him. Adam on the other hand was the opposite. Both Jamie and I were very aware that he had not so much had a one-on-one physical conversation with a girl, let alone anything more. I knew it made Jamie wince; maybe there was even a part of me too that found it embarrassing how he couldn't seem to form relationships with anyone. I didn't bring it up much to Jamie as a conversational topic, as much as I wanted to. I never really knew if Adam was listening or not. And I could imagine how he'd react if he heard Jamie and I discussing that of all things. I could imagine what he'd do. I found myself resisting the urge to shudder.

"Dean would be flabbergasted to think someone of the opposite sex was prepared to be seen dead with me," said Adam bitterly.

Jamie rolled his eyes.

"For crying out loud, will you change the record about Dean? Come on, if you're in a talking mood, get up those stairs and talk to Kayleigh! Arrange another date, make sure she knows you're interested."

Adam got up to his feet.

"I guess I could ask when she's next free, see if we can arrange something."

Jamie laughed.

"At long last, it looks like you're finally in possession of some gumption!"

I made the mistake of laughing. I registered Adam's face. He was furious; his face contorted into a ruthless snarl. I'd pay for that later. My heart thumped.

When he left, I leaned over to Jamie and said softly, "It always amazes me how you know exactly what to say to him. I just find him so…"

I waved my hands around, trying to find the right word.

"*Challenging.*"

It didn't seem like that choice of the word alone was enough. Jamie seemed to understand. He looped an arm around me.

"He's a hard nut to crack. I don't know, maybe it's a phase?"

We both looked knowingly at each other. This wasn't a temporary blip; a mere bump in the road. This was Adam's default setting; his lifelong phase.

We carried the dishes out to the kitchen sink. Jamie leaned against the counter, wanting to talk as I made a start on the washing-up.

"I'm going out tonight, by the way. Rachel's birthday drinks."

I looked at him puzzledly.

"I thought she'd already had her birthday party. Last Saturday, I remember."

Jamie rolled his eyes.

"You know what Rach is like - that was a celebration with her family. This is a celebration with her friends."

Jamie and Rachel had been together for nearly eighteen months now. She was stunningly beautiful; Jamie always joked that he felt that he was walking down the High Street with a supermodel whenever he was out with her, but I couldn't help but feel that beauty was only skin deep, myself. She's outwardly gorgeous: tall and lean with thick, golden hair that streamed down to her waist. She had huge eyes like Bambi and a little rosebud mouth permanently pursed into a pout. However, she had a precocious streak; naturally envious by nature, she required almost constant compliments and attention from Jamie. He seemed to think the world of her and it was blatant that she adored him, but I sometimes feared that he'd exhaust himself trying to make her permanently happy. And that's a task that is impossible for anyone, you can't singlehandedly serve in making someone happy all of the time, twenty-four hours a day.

"It won't turn into an all-nighter, will it, J?" I asked.

"I hate to sound like a nag but it's not the weekend and you've got work in the morning."

Jamie laughed.

"Well, this party animal will probably be back by around half ten, anyway. So, if you could have the hot cocoa and slippers ready by then, that would be great."

He laughed.

"God, that's a sentence that should never come out of a twenty-one-year-old's mouth."

Now

It's strange to think that there was once a time when I actively looked forward to having a bath. I used to excitedly plan which day of the week would be the evening where I would collapse into the house from work and grab a quick bite to eat before rushing upstairs to scrub off my make-up, scrape my hair back from my face and wash away the day. Often, I'd lie back, a facemask on, the bath so heaving with bubbles that they would practically be coming up beneath my chin. Sometimes, I'd shudder when I peered down at the marks on my arms and legs, which I consciously fought so hard *not* to look at most of the time. But most of the time, I was able to forget about what had caused me to end up with those marks. I could let my mind relax when I was in the bath; it seemed to be the one place where I could just truly be; without having endless thoughts swimming around my head; to the extent where my temple genuinely started to throb. It's unthinkable to me now that in the past, I could have easily spent an hour or two engulfed in bubbles, in utter bliss, before the raps at the bathroom door would start up: nine times out of ten, it would have been Jamie, wondering when I was planning on surfacing; when I was thinking of making a start on the dinner. I used to smile; laugh and tease him later as I prepared pasta, telling him he was hopeless at adulting and he was the only person I knew that couldn't master toast. I'd give anything to hear him ask me when dinner was ready now; to share a meal with him.

I felt a painful twinge in my chest. This happened to me a lot; pretty much all of the time really, as I thought of Jamie constantly. When it had first happened, I'd uttered a throwaway comment to Polly about having pains in my chest. I'd not expected her to do anything, but she surprisingly got herself worked up into a complete state. She was gasping and panting desperately, as though she'd had all of her oxygen snatched from her. She confided in me later that she'd panicked I was having a heart attack, brought on by all of the stress. This wasn't true. A doctor confirmed it. She came out to the house, which was rare, but Polly had obviously pleaded and pressed it on the phone. It was Doctor Keegan that came out. Jamie once said she looked like Madonna and I suppose she did really, except she wore linen shirts as opposed to latex. I remembered her lecturing Karen to stop smoking years ago; she droned on and on about the health risks. Two weeks later, Karen and I saw her in town, completely bladdered and smoking like Thomas the Tank Engine. Rather ironic. She had evidently had a cigarette or two before she came around to my house to check my chest. I remembered feeling momentarily distracted from my chest pains by the reek of her breath that stank so badly of coffee that I genuinely wondered whether she'd spooned instant coffee granules straight into her mouth before landing around. She looked at me with such palpable pity. The last time I had seen her, it had been to discuss the ongoing issues with Adam. I didn't wish to engage with her; I hated her for coming into my house; for daring to peer around; for her eyes briefly darting to the sympathy cards, as though she was fighting every urge to not simply saunter up and to read through all of the messages. Doctor Keegan confirmed that I was not experiencing heart issues and I could certainly be reassured that I wasn't having a heart attack. She stated in a rather bored tone of voice, that it looked as though I was simply suffering with heartache. It was often associated with grief; it was common enough, given what had occurred. She uttered this with no expression, perhaps heartache simply wasn't exciting enough for her to report as an ailment, as far as she could see. Polly flapped around her, practically kissing her feet. She kept saying, "Thank you, Doctor, thank you" as though she was in some sort of budget remake of *Doc Martin*. A doctor didn't need to tell me that my heart was broken. I knew full well that it had been smashed into smithereens.

I thought of Jamie; the vivacious, glorious Jamie that could make me smile the minute he walked in the room, despite not seemingly doing anything. It made absolutely no sense to me that the most alive person I had ever met in my life, that had literally seized every second of every day and who had always been as keen as mustard to experience every adventure that life had to offer, was suddenly not around anymore. I felt the twinge in my chest grow sharper; more piercing. I held my legs up to my chest; I leaned over my knees; becoming increasingly aware of the fact that I resembled a crumpled-up piece of paper lying there in a too-hot bath that made my skin look aggravated and sore. I was sick of looking at myself; I was sick of being me at that moment. I needed to go *back*.

I closed my eyes and sank beneath the water. I thought of Jamie; Jamie's from babyhood to adulthood dancing around my mind, seemingly within touching distance, but tauntingly so unattainable. Jamie: It was funny how we all just started calling him that as opposed to James. On Jamie's first day of primary school, Jamie met his best friend Max. Two peas in a pod from the word go, Max put his sticky little hand into Jamie's at the end of the day and said, "You're my best friend, Jamie." I thought this was so cute. I'd never really gone in for nicknames, but Jamie just seemed so fitting for my precious boy. It was cheeky, fun, and light-hearted; it suited Jamie to a tee. We'd never looked back. He'd been Jamie ever since. Until…until…

I sank down further beneath the water. I could feel it starting to seep into my ears. I knew I would need to come up for air soon, but there was time yet. Plenty of time. I needed to stay underwater; cancel out the outside world; stay in the past, where things were bearable. Jamie was alive then. Jamie was alive.

There was pounding at the door. I'm not supposed to slide the bolt across the door when I'm using the bathroom anymore; Polly didn't like it. She wanted it to be that I left it open at all times, so she'd be able to get to me if there was an emergency, if I needed anything. We both knew what she was so scared I was going to do if I actually had some time to myself in a locked room, without her lingering around me all the time; her presence resembling a jailor's. I had locked the door earlier after she'd suggested I had a bath. She thought it might make me feel a little more HUMAN again. I could just forget about the world around me for a half hour or so. Polly seemed to think I'd forget all about my dead child if I wallowed about happily like a hippo in a puddle for a while. She really is a mess. She so arrogantly assumes that she is the font of all knowledge, but she is in reality, a shining example of how not to do things. She kept banging at the door, it sounded like she was gearing up to put her shoulder to it. As amusing as it would have been to hear her try and do her best Vin Diesel impression, I was becoming increasingly aware that my chest was starting to feel unbearably tight. Panicked, I sat up in the water, desperately gasping for air. I felt as though I'd been shipwrecked and had been spat back on to the shore; dazed and decrepit.

Polly thumped harder and harder on the door. She wasn't going to have any skin left on her knuckles at this rate. Good. At least it would mean that she'd have to stop pestering me; haranguing me 24/7. She begged me to open the door. It sounded as though she was on the verge of tears.

I found it strange hearing Polly plead to see me; marooned pathetically on the other side of the door. It seemed to be the literal embodiment of the wedge that had been between us for years. With it just being the two of us, I was desperate to have a close relationship with her; a sister I could confide in; meet up with; trust implicitly. It was just never the case. I went through the motions; lied smoothly to other people, and claimed we were like two birds of a feather. We were forever having meet-ups: coffee dates in the day at cosy coffee shops overrun with women with sleek, styled hair whose biggest dilemma that day is over what Frappuccino to buy; shopping trips where we both spend too much and urge the other to go for whatever wicked treat it was that took our fancy; evenings spent at one of our houses, sipping wine and letting off steam. Having a whinge about that cow from work. Venting about bills. Gushing about the kids. I became so good at creating an idyllic relationship with the perfect sister. I willed it to be true so badly, but the bottom line is, it wasn't. The hard fact of the matter is that if I hadn't had the kids, Polly and I probably would have lost contact years ago. Polly had always had a tumultuous relationship with our mum, so given that my dad was no longer around and it had just been Mum living at the family home on her own for all of those years, she wasn't exactly a regular visitor, so it wouldn't have been a case that we were constantly bumping into each other there. The true irony is that Polly's own apartment is only about a five-minute drive from my house but there wasn't naturally a major inclination for us to see one another. I was desperate for Polly to be a present Aunt for Jamie and Adam. I wanted her to be loving; attentive; warm. Polly wasn't naturally maternal and she had always struggled with young children. She would pick facials over finger-painting, one-night stands over cosy pyjamaed evenings, any day of the week. She frequently exclaimed on the rare occasions that she did stop by, with seemingly no ulterior motives, that she couldn't believe I could be so content with such a boring, *empty* life.

The kids were handy when she wanted to pose around at the petting zoo or at the activity centre every once and a while, tagging along with her married friends, who all had broods of their own at this stage. Polly enjoyed Jamie's cuteness and charm; she enjoyed holding on to his hand as he dazzled everyone; making them smile; making them laugh. She could even muddle along with Adam as she had the peace of mind that it was only for a short burst. I craved for her to want to be an active sister, an active Aunt for so long. I made a point out of making a massive deal out of her birthday and at Christmas; despite the fact that it became a yearly tradition that she'd *forget* to get anything for myself and the kids on our respective special days. I made a point of calling her every week for years; always on a Sunday morning as I drank my coffee on the window-seat. She'd be airy and distracted; aloofly brag about some new man she was seeing; some promotion at work. She was always most comfortable talking about her favourite subject: herself. I'd start to prattle on about the kids and what they were up to. She'd um and aah for a second; offer up half-baked praise and make her excuses; desperate to slip away. It was pretty revealing that it's now of all times when my world has concaved, that she suddenly wants to be in my pocket; when she can't spend enough time with me. It's a tiring job for Polly Pocket, playing the devoted sister, day after day, night after night, with there being no set date for her final performance to be taking place.

She kept knocking on the door and calling. I let her.

Then

I edged my way across the landing. I found it humiliating to admit that the knot in my stomach, which was always there to some extent whenever Adam was around had tightened to the degree where I found myself really resisting the urge to double over in pain. But I knew the longer I left it, the worse it would become. He'd had a good ninety minutes; two hours now to sit upstairs and brood. He was worse when he'd had time to plot; to hatch. He'd make things far more difficult. I conceded that it was better to face the music now; to strike whilst the iron was still hot, so to speak. Time to rip that Band-Aid off, no matter how much it stung.

I crept up to his closed bedroom door. I hovered for a minute, shamelessly stalling. I ran a hand through my hair nervously, before giving a rapid rat-a-tat-tat on the door. There was no response.

"Adam, love, it's me."

There was silence. He was angry.

"Adam, love, this won't take long. Am I okay to just come in for a second?"

He didn't utter a peep. He wanted me to squirm. The strain had started to churn inside me; I felt a crippling sense of nausea.

"Adam, sweetheart, can I just have a quick word with you?"

There was a noise from the other side of the door. Muffled, but a noise all the same. I decided to interpret this as a green light to open the door. I gingerly poked my head around and saw Adam sitting cross-legged on his bed. He looked so *young* for his age. He was nearing eighteen and yet he easily could have passed for about fourteen. I'd really worried about Adam in the past, I'd fretted that there might be something wrong, as he didn't appear to have started puberty by the time, he was sixteen. I took him to the doctor; genuinely concerned and was told by a man whose lips were so thin, that they periodically practically disappeared into his face, that Adam was simply a *late bloomer*. It was slightly unusual that his voice had not begun to break, even slightly, at the age he was at, but it wasn't anything that he felt majorly alarmed by. He had advised Adam and I to simply be patient. He'd told Adam gruffly that before he knew it, he'd be a big, hairy man with a voice as deep as the ocean. I think that he'd interpreted Adam's expressionlessness as suppressed mortification. That's why when we were leaving, he had said to Adam in what I think he thought to be a reassuring manner, "Don't stress about all of this, Adam. You just focus on your studies, getting those GCSEs under your belt. If nothing's changed in a year, we can think about increasing your testosterone levels, to see if that does the trick." It's strange, I'm no biologist but I would have thought that a lack of testosterone would have meant that Adam would have possessed a lack of aggression. That certainly wasn't the case, not with me, anyway.

Adam ostentatiously rolled his eyes like marbles upon my entry. He stared at me sullenly for a couple of seconds; undeniably ominous and odious. I found myself silently groaning. I wished I'd never come into his room. I wished that I'd just been able to leave him to it. But I knew that he'd be so vexed if he felt that he'd been sidelined; segregated. He hated being ostracised. He was a loner at school; he drifted around on his own all the time like a sad little ghoul. When Jamie was at school, people left Adam alone, as no one wanted to rock the boat with Jamie. He'd been top dog in every social situation since he was knee-high to a grasshopper so nobody wanted to run the risk of ending up falling out of favour with him; becoming alienated. However, Jamie had left school at seventeen after deciding that A-Levels weren't for him. He went down the Apprenticeship route instead; wound up getting his gig at the garage. He loved it there; he was happy; got on like a house on fire with Dave and Kev, the other men that worked there. Good news for Jamie: bad news for Adam. Without Jamie's presence to keep him protected, people at school were far more inclined now to give Adam a piece of their mind. They said he gave them the heebie-jeebies; the creeps. They claimed that he recorded private conversations of people who hadn't even noticed he was in the room; that he took photographs of people without their knowledge. It was as though he wanted some sort of unsettling log of all of them and their lives, without contributing anything positive whatsoever to the year-group himself.

Academia was Adam's saving grace in a lot of senses. He was extremely intelligent; he practically had a meltdown if he didn't score full marks in any test. He got the best GCSE results in his school's history; he's on course to scoop the top A-Level results too. His teachers think he should aim high, head to

Cambridge or Oxford. He's smart enough to win a coveted place at a really prestigious university. I'd tried to ask Adam loads of times what he'd like to do, as I hated the thought of him feeling forced to go down the academic path, in case this was the last thing he wanted and he felt like it was simply, *expected* of him. Adam never spoke to me about it, he preferred to keep me in the dark.

He stared down at his phone when he seemed satisfied that he'd induced enough discomfort. It was easier to speak to him when I wasn't actually being looked at him in the eye.

"Did you hear me knocking, sweetheart?" I asked. I heard the wobble in my voice and hated myself for it. He smirked.

"I did," he said dryly.

I decided to plough on, but I was at the end of my tether.

"I just wanted to speak to you about Dean, darling. It really saddens me that you think he's disappointed with you; that you never lived up to his expectations. That's not true, Dean thinks you're great. A really interesting young man."

Adam glared at me.

"Jamie said earlier that Dean thinks I'm interesting," he interjected coolly.

I felt thrown.

"Did he?" I said, taken aback.

Adam resembled a snake uncoiling itself.

"Interesting is a kind way of saying that Dean clearly thinks I'm as exciting as watching paint dry. It's funny how he never described JAMIE as interesting. Dean always thought he was laugh-a-minute, the life and soul."

He looked livid.

"He thought the world of Jamie. When you and him were together. You'd have thought that THEY were father and son. Jamie was the son Dean always wanted, he made that perfectly plain."

I tucked my hair behind my ears.

"I know that Dean didn't exactly take the gong for Dad of the year but there's no point in getting so worked up about it all. You just need to concentrate on the fact that your future looks so promising; you've got so much excitement in the pipeline. You just need to keep your eye on the prize; focus on getting those grades that everybody knows you're capable of. The world's your oyster, Adam."

Adam's lip was curled so much, it looked like it was practically coming up to his eyebrow.

“Will you shut it about the exams? Stop trying to change the subject. Back to Dean.”

He grabbed my arm.

“He could pull his socks up when he wanted though, couldn’t he? He was all-singing, all-fucking dancing whenever Jamie was concerned!”

His fingernails were digging right into my arm. He’d always dig into my skin until he made the skin pierce slightly; he’d never stop until he induced at least a whimper. He got visible enjoyment out of seeing me in pain; at his mercy. I let out a small yelp subserviently. I was certain that would make him stop. I was wrong.

“Why do you always try and gloss over the fact that I am the black sheep of this family, the dead weight, the *nobody*? Why do you bother trying to pretend that you and everybody else don’t view me as the GHOST brother, the one who never quite lives up to the first? Do you know how fucking hard that is?”

He gave me an agonising Chinese burn; he smirked as I winced.

“You really are a stupid bitch, you know. A really stupid fucking bitch.”

He went to pull my hair; I knew this routine. He’d do it until he had at least a tuft of it in his hands. He would then look at me with revulsion; ask me why I’d push him so far. He would demand that I change; I brought out the worse in him. Stupid women like me don’t make natural mothers. We need to be whipped into shape; taught from scratch. We’re utterly moronic when left to our own devices. We needed to be under a strict dictatorship at all times.

Adam leapt to his feet and pinned one of my arms behind my back; shoved me against the wall. Despite looking so puny and pathetic; there had been times in the past when I had really thought that he might hurl me out of the window in a blind rage. The red mist seemed to descend upon him; the monster was released. I couldn’t fathom how he could show such casual cruelty. And then merely discard me after he had grown bored with tormenting me; expect me to go off and to busy myself cooking his meals and laundering his clothes until I was summoned again. It wasn’t always a grab or a throw or a pinch or a push. It was when he didn’t do anything that was worse. When he’d look me up and down; weigh up if he could be bothered to think up a new form of cruelty with which to show me. Sometimes he’d smile and laugh, ask me about my day, suggest we go and see a film one weekend, and spend the day together. That’s worse. Because I see what he could have been like if only he’d tried harder. But that’s not a part that he’s prepared to play too often: the normal son.

Jamie didn't know. He knew that Adam was surly, confusing, and unspeakably trying company to be around. But he didn't know what he said or did when he was out of earshot; when it was just him and I. I couldn't stand the thought of him knowing. I feared the truth would devastate him; crush him. It was too awful and atrocious a truth for anyone to have to shoulder; let alone someone like Jamie, whom I wanted to protect from everything.

Adam had been hissing at me venomously; looking like a depraved serpent. I was shocked that the huge vein that engulfed his forehead hadn't yet popped. It always pulsed alarmingly out of his brow when he was angry, making me think that it was going to burst at the drop of a hat. Sometimes, I wondered if that would be for the best. No, I didn't really think that. Did I?

Suddenly the words, "What the hell is going on in here?" burst into the room.

I spun round, feeling weak with relief. Unbeknown to me, at some point or another, Jamie had crept in and had witnessed Adam in action.

"Why the hell were you hissing at my mum?" Jamie boomed at Adam. He looked as though he wanted to swing for him. I peered anxiously at Adam. He was in victim mode; hanging his head, appearing meek and knock-kneed. His default setting, whenever in doubt. The victim. I was afraid of Jamie really losing it. I was furious at myself for doing so, but I went into peace-making mode seamlessly.

"He was just a little het up, Jamie. Adam's still struggling to process Dean not being around for him. He doesn't mean any harm by it, he's just pretty poor at staying in touch, always has been. But he's not a bad old stick, really. Not in the slightest."

Jamie wasn't buying it.

"How *dare* you speak to my mum like dirt!" he raged; his fury undeniable. Adam quivered.

"You pathetic little freak. Standing there, bellowing at my mum. You're a vile little loser. You stand there and snivel, you're not getting any more airtime."

Adam wept, practically sinking to his knees. Jamie brushed past him; his intolerance was as plain as day.

"Come on, Mum. He deserves to be on his own."

I scurried after Jamie. He slammed Adam's bedroom door shut with a bang. The house practically shook.

"Don't you dare think about coming out of there until I say!" he roared. Adam sobbed from the other side of the door.

Jamie and I went downstairs in silence. At the bottom of the stairs, without saying a word, he wrapped me up in a huge hug.

I knew there was so much he wanted to say; so much that he wanted to ask, but I insisted into his shoulder that we'd talk about it all in the morning; he could ask me anything he wanted then. But for now, he was to go out and have an amazing night with Rachel and his friends.

Jamie said firmly that he'd cancel; I needed him more. I insisted that he went out and enjoyed himself; painted the town red. He looked at me.

"I will be back by ten, okay?" he said as he hugged me tightly.

"And promise you'll call me if you need anything. And leave *him*. He's made his bed, let him lie in it."

Jamie took off. I watched him from the living room window; striding up to his clump of friends waiting in the corner. They laughed uproariously as they hugged and joked. I missed seeing them take off around the corner. I was Googling on my phone, *domestic abuse from my son.*

I felt a shiver down my spine. I turned slowly around. Adam was standing in the doorway. He cracked his knuckles. I felt my heart pound in my chest. Jamie wasn't there. It was just him and I.

He looked at me as though I sickened him. One long, loathsome look before slinking upstairs again. I bit my lip and waited a few moments before moving again. I turned on the TV. I glanced at the clock on the mantelpiece. 7:23 pm. I sighed. Not long until Jamie came back.

Now

I sat on my bed, feeling cocooned in my dressing gown. Three days after Jamie died, Polly bought me a huge, quilted towelling dressing gown that made me feel as though I was being smothered by countless duvets. It was thick and pink and I was extremely self-conscious of resembling the pink panther. I sat on my bed; my hair looked a complete mess. I found it unbelievable to think that before Jamie died; I used to constantly prioritise looking presentable. I would never have dreamed of leaving the house without my makeup immaculately applied, my hair sitting glossily and neatly in its bouncy bob, and wouldn't have considered leaving the house, without having my heeled boots clacking beneath me. When the kids were young, I had dived around in trainers all the time; it was easier. I'd have fallen on my neck if I'd decided to totter around in stilettoed boots at the playpark. However, as they'd got older, I'd tried to make a little more effort to look my best; it made me feel good about myself. This felt like a lifetime ago. I couldn't believe that I'd once been able to bustle around my room; genuinely spending a few minutes musing over which blouse to wear, which shoes, deliberating over which would look best. It all seems so trivial now, so pointless.

I looked across my room. Sitting beneath my dressing table was a pair of ludicrously high stilettoed heels. I didn't buy them for myself, I'd never have dreamed of buying such a ridiculous pair of shoes. No, my friend Karen gave them to me for the Christmas just gone. She'd had a tiff with her husband Geoff and she'd decided to get her own back on him by treating her and me to some designer heels on his credit card. At least mine were a practical enough colour, a treacle black, but towering at a statuesque six inches in height. Karen's were an electric neon pink. She thought they were brilliant. She called them her, *hooker heels*. She always said she had never been bold enough to wear them at the age when she could have easily got away with them, so she had decided to grow old disgracefully. I looked at my black heels, the one and only time that I had worn them was at Jamie's 21st. He'd told me that I looked a million dollars and made a point of dancing around with me for ages; even though there was a roomful of his nearest and dearest, all desperate to have some one-on-one time with him themselves. Polly had suggested to me the other day that I wore those heels to the funeral, she thought it might be nice if we all made an effort to dress to the nines. Jamie would have liked it. I remembered throwing the heels at her head, I missed, unfortunately. Still, she got the message to get out of my range. The audacity of her, she seemed to be under the impression that she could simply treat Jamie's funeral as some sort of fashion parade and that I somehow wasn't going to react. As if I was going to stagger around in silly tarty heels that would look absurd on anyone over the age of twenty-four, at my own son's funeral. Polly really did just judge everyone by her own standards. Which, let's face it, are so low at the best of times, that you could trip over them.

I suppose in so many ways, Karen had always been like more of a sister to me than Polly. She had always had my back. I had always been someone to hold the belief that it was more important to have a sprinkle of friends that you truly cherished, as opposed to dozens and dozens of breezy, artificial *friendships*, where you never quite seemed to scratch the surface, one way or another. Karen had been my closest friend since I was about thirteen. We had navigated the minefield of secondary school together as a twosome; a little tag team. We had always been pretty different in some respects. Karen had never been particularly bothered about the whole marriage-and-babies thing. However, things changed for her when she met Geoff, she could really see herself having a future with him. He suddenly made the thought of building a life with someone and having a family seem so exciting; seen so *necessary*. Karen fell pregnant with her and Geoff's first child after having only dated him for a few months. I remembered us both being elated, that as best friends, we were both expecting our first child at the same time. Karen had really posed as a rock to me during Tom's illness. She was dumbfounded that I never crumbled, in the weeks after Tom's death, when Jamie was only a tiny baby. I vividly remembered cradling a very contended Jamie in my arms whilst she frenziedly tried to soothe her wailing baby daughter Tilly. I remembered her turning to me and saying as she looked the personification of frazzled, "I just don't know how you manage. You're my heroine, Suze. *I'm* on my bloody knees, and that's with having an extra pair of hands in Geoff to help. You're a flipping superhero."

Jamie and Tilly were in the same school year. We'd always thought this was really nice. Jamie had always been bright and vibrant; always resembling a little lovebird in amongst a flock of pigeons. Tilly had always been painfully shy; she flushed peony if she was spoken to, she whispered when she talked, and she was teased mercilessly at school. Jamie took on the role of her full-time protector; he was so patient and nurturing towards her. She always trailed around after him, a pensive expression on her face. Usually, Tilly could only really be described as a broken doll. She walked around with her head hanging; her neck was so thin it looked as though her head was going to snap off it at any moment and she had a jumpy, fraught walk that always made her look like a puppet who was being pulled erratically. Jamie refused to stand by if she was being ridiculed; he pulled the catty girls aside, and made it clear that all the name-calling and jostling that took place, was to stop. Every girl in the year had jeered, *Silly Tilly* at her before then, she was seen as the laughing stock, the butt of every joke. Jamie soon had that nipped in the bud. He even took her as his date to the school prom and treated her like a complete and utter princess. Rachel, who'd wistfully longed to be with Jamie for years at this stage, was practically green with envy, Max had told me. Jamie really treated Tilly like she was special. He wanted her to have at least one evening in her life when she felt amazing and was waited on hand and foot by a Prince Charming. What's really strange is, and as unkind as this sounds, Tilly had never been *pretty*. She had always been plain; she had a long, pale face and lank hair that hung in rats' tails down her back. But on the Prom night, Tilly really did look beautiful. When she took Jamie's arm, she truly did look a vision. That was the magic of Jamie though, he always seemed to sprinkle a little bit of sparkle wherever he went, so you felt like the best version of yourself around him. It takes someone very special indeed to touch people's lives like that.

Karen always joked that "We learnt from Cinderella that a night out and a new pair of shoes can change a girl's life." I think she'd always wistfully hoped that Jamie and Tilly would end up together. Karen had always been optimistic.

I talked to Karen a lot, we'd always had an upfront friendship. Karen and I had sat many times on either her sofa or mine, a cup of tea in hand, as we talked about anything and everything. Karen had frequently confided in me that she worried so much about Tilly's passiveness; she'd so hoped it would be a phase, whereas it was obviously becoming quite the permanent fixture in her personality. She'd voice that her instinct screamed that Geoff wasn't okay with their son Greg wanting to pursue his long-held ambition of ballet as a career.

Geoff had always wanted a relationship with his son that resembled the tight-knit bond he'd shared with his own father. He had longed to have a son that he could go-kart with at the weekends; go on fishing trips with; avidly follow the football with. Geoff had desperately tried to find common ground with Greg since he'd been a small boy, but there had always been a sense of both of them struggling to relate to one another. On the other hand, Karen had always found Greg so much easier to bond with. He was gregarious and exuberant – everything that Tilly wasn't. Geoff didn't acknowledge his difficulty to build a bond with Greg; he preferred not to speak about it, he didn't like it being addressed. Karen had always felt resented. Greg, like his mother, had always adored the Arts and Geoff felt that Karen had manipulated him into acting in as theatrical a manner as possible. Geoff had always found Greg's dramatic nature to be grating. Karen had always encouraged him to express himself from when he was no age. He used to leap around in fairy wings in front of Karen and I putting on, *shows*, us his captive audience, that applauded wildly when he curtseyed wobblily at the end.

Karen knew that I struggled with Adam. I told her about his calculated personality; how I constantly felt like he was conspiring against me. She didn't really get it properly until he was a teenager. Karen had always perceived him to be shy, untalkative, and introverted. But as she saw how he behaved as a teenager, she did voice to me on a couple of occasions that on the teenager front, "It's the quiet ones that you definitely need to watch out for." I told Karen about the way he'd speak to me, the dreadful names he'd call me, that sometimes I felt had stuck to me like tar. She was stunned; she never realised he could be so horrid. She was truly appalled when I told her about how he'd grab me, how he'd turn at the drop of a hat, about all of the malicious treatments he reserved solely for me. She was the one that said he was disturbed, twisted, unhinged. *She* was the one that had dubbed him a narcissist! Karen had actually mused aloud if he was actually *beyond* help, given how long all of this had been going on for. She had urged me to visit the doctor, to ask for help.

Speaking of help, Karen had messaged me umpteen times to ask if I wanted her to bring around milk, bread, or any staples whatsoever. She'd messaged to ask me if I wanted her to come around. I was more than welcome to come to hers whenever. I was to turn up anytime I fancied. I was f*amily*, after all. But she'd not physically come around once. I couldn't help but feel wounded. When Greg was beaten to a pulp by some cruel bullies outside of the school, wild horses wouldn't have stopped me from racing around to Karen's, to show my support; to see if there was anything I could do. Jamie ended up being the one to teach those bullies a lesson, anyway.

As if on cue, a message landed through from Karen.

It read, *"Hi, Susanna. I really do have no clue as to what to say to you. Words really do fail me. I have always been a big believer in what doesn't kill you makes you stronger, so I want you to know, that as bleak as things now seem, you and dear Adam will get through this, xx."*

I threw my phone across the room. It cracked. I didn't care. It looked how I felt, fractured and changed and unfixable.

I was seething, she of all people had referred to Adam directly and hadn't even mentioned Jamie!

I shuffled to my wardrobe and pulled out a bottle of wine I'd concealed there a few days earlier. I'd bid my time and had been able to strike when Polly was taking the bins out. I felt consumed with self-disgust. I started glugging.

Then

I had been dozing lightly all evening. I couldn't seem to concentrate on anything on the TV for too long. I flicked through countless channels before eventually ending up throwing the remote to one side and scrolling through my phone. I checked to see if I had any new messages. Karen had sent me a video of a parrot belting out a Rihanna song. I chuckled, she was forever sending me stuff like that; particularly when I was at work. My Admin job frequently felt as boring as sin, so a video of a monkey dancing or a dog saying, "I love you", could really serve in making the job seem a little bit more bearable. I checked to see if Polly had got back to the message, I'd sent her that morning; asking if she fancied getting lunch together that week. It felt like it had been an absolute age since we had spoken. She'd read it but hadn't yet replied. I sighed, *that seemed rather rude*. I scanned through my texts with Polly, I had actually sent her nine messages in a row but she had failed to get back to any of them. I frequently mused over whether she would ever actually think to contact me of her own accord if I decided to stop being the person to reach out first all of the time. It was fast becoming tiring.

I was just starting to watch a programme; a detective thriller when a message pinged through. Assuming it was Jamie checking in, I reached over to peer at it. It wasn't Jamie. It was Polly.

She said, *"Yeah, whatever, lunch sounds okay. It may have to be in a few weeks or so though. It's manic with me just now. I don't suppose Jamie would be able to pop out to my place tomorrow just to take a look at my car? It's playing up again, it's the thorn in my side at the moment. Love having a mechanic in the family. If he could check it out before 5 pm tomorrow, that would be great. Take care Px."*

I sighed. Polly only ever really seemed to get in contact when she was looking for a favour. If the boot was on the other foot, she'd have no qualms whatsoever about declining to help me with the tiniest of favours, but she knew that I struggled to say no, particularly if someone was in a crisis. After all, Polly did need her car. I mulled over messaging Jamie; to ask if there was any chance of him popping out to look at it before he began work at the garage tomorrow. I typed out the message and then deleted it. No, it was unfair of me to interrupt his night. He shouldn't always have to be the crusader; the hero rescuing everyone else. Jamie deserved to let his hair down, and have a brilliant time celebrating his girlfriend's birthday. I toyed with the idea of punching out a response to Polly and thought better of it. I couldn't be bothered, to be quite honest. So, I left my mobile to one side and ended up settling back into the detective programme. It was fast-paced and furious, I was left feeling tired *watching* it. I knew it was the kind of programme that Jamie would like; he loved all those heart-stopping thrillers, he was brilliant at cracking all the codes and working out who the killers were. I recorded it for him, he could watch it tomorrow. I closed my eyes, suddenly exhausted. I snuggled down onto the sofa, my eyelids feeling like heavy weights.

I woke up with a start to the sound of my mobile ringing, insistently trilling. I glanced at the clock, I assumed that I'd only been asleep for a couple of minutes, but looked as though it had been for over two hours. Bloody hell. I saw it was Rachel calling. Confused, I rubbed my eyes and tried to sound awake.

"Hello?" I said blearily.

I heard her sobbing. Rachel's always been a weepy drunk. I assumed that she'd gone a bit overboard with her birthday drinks and was perhaps a little overly emotional. I was a bit puzzled that she'd called me, of all people. We had an okay relationship, but we'd never really spoken that much without Jamie being there. I wondered if they'd had a falling out. She kept saying his name over and over again, and then dissolving into sobs. The lovebirds had clearly had a falling out of some kind. I tried to think of something consoling that I could say to her.

"Rachel, lovie, there's no need to cry so. I'm sure it's just a silly misunderstanding, a mistake. You'll sort it in the morning, I'm sure it will all be all right."

Rachel carried on crying; she sounded hysterical, demonic. She'd always been slightly on the melodramatic side, acting like the world had ended if she and Jamie had the slightest disagreement. Still, this was dramatic with bells on, even for her.

"Rachel, why don't you put Jamie on the phone? I'd like to speak with him. Can you do that for me, please? Rachel? *Rachel*?"

She burst into a fresh batch of tears. There was so much background noise; so much movement around her. I couldn't work out if she was inside or outside.

"I can't," she said tearfully, eventually.

"I can't put Jamie on the phone. He's dead," she gasped, before sobbing uncontrollably.

I felt cold, shivery, and shaky. I felt completely floored. Just for a moment.

"I can tell my J's put you up to this, Rachel. He's a prankster, I know. Next time, just humour him by pretending you'll prank call me. Honestly, what a sick joke, eh!"

She started to burble; she sounded crazed and erratic. She started jabbering manically, words like, "thug", "confrontation", and "knife", ringing in my ears. It felt like my head was being held underwater. I couldn't listen to it anymore.

"That's enough of all of that nonsense, Rachel. Stop all of that malarkey. Now, go off and enjoy the rest of your birthday. I'll call Jamie myself, okay?"

I cut the call. I felt eerily calm. Rachel was drunk; she wasn't thinking or indeed talking straight. She was all over the place; perhaps Jamie had grown tired of how demanding and self-absorbed she was and had decided to end the relationship. Yes, that would be it. The second birthday celebration would have been the final straw. He'd have looked around and suddenly it would have dawned on him: there's more to life than sitting here with this egotistical brat and all her hanger-ons. He'd have pulled her tactfully aside; he'd have apologised for hurting her but he would have said that it just wasn't working out. They were too different; he just didn't feel that they were a good match for each other anymore. Then he'd have left, he wouldn't want to have given her any mixed messages. Jamie has always been honourable. Rachel would have felt bitter; vexed, and discarded. She would have sat there all evening with her witch's coven, discussing how best to dole out some payback. "Revenge is a dish best served cold", that's the kind of comment that she would have relished saying. She would have seen it as appropriate revenge to call me up; to pretend he was dead, just because she was incensed that he'd woken up and had smelt the coffee, realised that he could do better than her.

Rachel could have quite the forked tongue when she wanted. Karen had filled me in on some of the catty put-downs that she used to throw Tilly's way, when they were at school, when Jamie wasn't around.

“You really could do with a bit of concealer, lip-liner, and mascara, Tilly. You’re so pasty and I think it would just give you a little more *life*, babe. The other girls think you look dug up. I just don’t want you to constantly look like the drab little loser. You’re just giving them ammunition. I mean, you want the teasing to stop, don’t you?”

Calculated and abrasive…that was Rachel’s stye. Venom disguised as honey – as if I was going to take on board anything she said now, as the deserted ex. “*Hell hath no fury like a woman scorned.*” Yes, that summed up Rachel to the nth degree.

I tried to call Jamie. I wanted to let him know what had just happened, the loathsome low blow from Rachel. He needed to be armed, he needed to be prepared. I’d ask him what had finally made him think he couldn’t be with her anymore and then he’d come home and I’d make him a hot chocolate, the way I used to do when he was little and down in the dumps. We’d have a good long chat about it all and I’d hug him and reassure him that we sometimes have to kiss the odd frog or so, but that it will all be worth it because he will soon meet his perfect love, the one that makes everything better. I listened to his phone ring. I frowned; he was normally good at picking up his phone. I tried to relax, he’d be busy, that’s all. Maybe he’d called up some of his friends, they’d decided to make a bit of a night of it. I didn’t want to intrude. He’d ring me back at the earliest chance he’d get. I just needed to be patient.

I didn’t really know what to do with myself. I wriggled around on the sofa, feeling like a spare part. I walked around the room and sat down. I tried to distract myself with my phone, and I tried to focus on the TV again once more. I was watching some talk show repeat; the interviewee was laughing. The sound was siren-like, it seemed to wriggle its way into every squiggle of my brain. There was something strangely ominous about it; it made me feel uncomfortable. Then the landline began to ring. I instinctively frowned, no one ever really called that anymore. Max did occasionally, he usually phoned on that when he knew Jamie was at work and I’d be home. He’d pick my brains about birthday and Christmas presents. I always thought it endearing that he went to such lengths to keep the gifts a surprise, he could have easily have just asked me what Jamie was after when it was just him and I in the room when he popped around. Max was always nipping around, it was strange for him not to make an appearance every other day or so. Jamie and him were inseparable, a real double act. I thought the world of him too. He had such a good heart. Max had had a really tough beginning, his home life had been hard, but he'd always been a part of this family. I thought nothing of him being around all the time. He just fitted in. I'd always felt a far greater kinship with him than with Adam.

I froze as the landline blared on, shrieking and insistent. Perturbed, I rose tentatively from the sofa and made my way over to the phone on the little hallway table, wobblily. My hands shook as I picked it up and brought it to my ear.

I let out a long, shuddering breath that I had been unaware that I'd been holding.

"Hello?" I said hoarsely.

"Hey, Susanna."

It *was* Max. His voice was thick, as though he had a heavy cold.

"Are you okay, Max?" I asked, concerned.

"You don't sound too well, darling. Are you under the weather?"

He sniffled slightly.

"No, no, I'm not ill, Susanna. I'm so sorry that I wasn't the one to tell you first. I think you and Rachel got cut off when she was speaking with you. I was with the Police, it's all so…"

He broke down in tears. I gripped the hallway table. Max wasn't a crier; it took an awful lot for him to even admit that he was *sad.*

"Susanna, I'm so sorry to have to tell you this, but it's J, it's our J. He's dead."

I stood motionlessly. My legs suddenly buckled; I felt like I was falling from a great height. I dropped to the floor, clinging to the phone. Max heard the thud and sounded panicked.

"Susanna, are you okay? Please speak to me, have you fallen?"

I sniffed fiercely and tried to rid my voice of the exceptionally irritating wobble that had crept into it.

"Of course, Jamie's not dead. I would know."

I gathered momentum, and I sounded more defiant.

"I would know if he was, Max, I would know."

Max started babbling. It was white noise; I couldn't take any of it in. He burbled on about an investigation, they were questioning all these witnesses, himself included. It didn't feel real. He sounded like one of those characters on the detective programme I'd been watching earlier, he didn't sound like him. This lingo wasn't Max's. His words were the kind that were plucked straight from a fast-paced drama. I refused to let myself listen to it; it wasn't true, it wasn't true, it wasn't true.

I refused to accept that something so catastrophic could have happened to the person I loved most in the world and I could have been none-the-wiser. If my Jamie was dying, I'd have *known*. A mother's intuition it's one of the most powerful forces around. If my Jamie was lying dying; I'd have felt a sledgehammer hit my heart; I wouldn't have been lying on the sofa, dozing like a cat as the TV blared obliviously on. I wouldn't have woken up, still in the dark. If it had been true, I'd have woken up and would have emotionally collapsed. But I hadn't; that hadn't happened so it couldn't be true. I wasn't like Max's mother; she was drugged up to her eyeballs most of the time; she lay in bed all day, out of action. She never gave a stuff about Max; she allowed me to practically bring her son up. As long as he was out of her hair, she wasn't bothered. I wasn't a remiss Mother; I was as present as present could be; I loved Jamie more than life itself. So, I would know if he'd lost his life. I would. I *would.*

I started to think that if I tapped the table a certain number of times; if I counted backwards from eight hundred in threes without stumbling or getting distracted, it would all turn out to be a malignant mistake. Jamie would be fine; he'd walk in that door again, larger than life and laughing. I was counting like my life depended on it. I'd always been good at Maths but I counted back – eight hundred, seven hundred and ninety-seven, seven hundred and ninety-four. I was counting; I could do it, it was working, I knew it.

Max's voice interrupted me.

"I am really sorry, Susanna," he said, his voice cracking.

That was it. There was something about hearing his voice as he said those words that made it register. I screamed into my knees, Max talking all the while. He was trying to coax and to console me, but there was nothing that could be said to make things better. Adam appeared, like the grim reaper. He skulked down the stairs. He wrenched the phone from my hands. He looked briefly as though the floor was rolling beneath his feet, Max was clearly telling him what had happened.

Adam began to weep.

"Jamie's dead. He was stabbed, and he was pronounced dead at the scene."

He leaned down to me; he attempted to hold me but I pushed him away.

"I want my boy, I want my boy," I sobbed.

He beamed momentarily; it was a wolfish grin.

"I'm here, Mum, I'm here!" he hissed.

"Get away from me!" I screeched, flailing at him. He looked stunned. I never lost my temper.

"I want my ACTUAL son, my Jamie!"

I waved him away, my distress palpable. He made for the stairs.

"I'll start making the calls. I'll ring Aunt Polly, let her know."

I lay on the floor, clutching my knees, anguished. I felt in physical agony.

Now

I sat on the edge of my bed. It was so strange, before Jamie died, I never spent that much time in my bedroom at all. I literally just used it to sleep in really. Otherwise, I was always in the kitchen or the living room, for the most part. Now, however, it felt like this was one of the only rooms in my own house I could be in without feeling like my head was constantly being pecked at. Polly always seemed to be hanging about like a bad smell; lingering incessantly and making me endless cups of tea, despite the fact that I never asked her to make me them and I very rarely drank so much as a sip from one. She'd watch me let one cup go stone cold and would then pick it up deftly and toss it down the sink before making me another one as she whistled jauntily. Polly was evidently on autopilot, it was ridiculous that she would actually look strangely unfinished to me now if she didn't have a cup of tea to hand at all times. In all of the years I'd known her, I couldn't ever recall her having made me a cup of tea. Ever. Rather ironic, really, when it seems to be all that she did now.

I'd had a bath earlier. I hadn't locked the door; I'd respected Polly's wishes. I had thought that because I'd done as she'd asked, she would have pushed off downstairs and left me alone. No such luck. She had hovered outside the whole time, listening in. I'd shouted at her to go away; I couldn't relax properly when she was lurking around outside. I asked her to go downstairs; she could make herself useful and load up the dishwasher or mop the kitchen floor. She seemed to think that I wanted her out of the way so I could end things. She barged right into the bathroom, despite the fact that I was lying there stark naked. I yelled at her to leave and she just stood there, hands on her hips and told me that she wasn't going anywhere. I accused her of being a female *Peeping Tom*. and made it clear that she was to get out of my sight, sharpish. Polly told me calmly that she was sorry I felt so aggravated, but she had reason to believe that I was having suicidal thoughts and as a result, she wasn't taking any chances. She'd then burst into tears and begged me to open up to her, she said she felt sick with fear that she was going to come up and find me…

She'd never finish that sentence but we both knew what it was. *Dead.* Polly had become increasingly panicked about finding me dead after having visited Jamie. Well, Jamie's body.

It had all been a blur; the most ungodly, heinous blur I think anyone could ever face in a lifetime. Detectives had been calling me up; they had explained that Jamie's body was still unavailable to be released for a funeral, as it was currently still being used as evidence. *Evidence*, it's not a word that you think you'll ever hear being used to describe your child. It's so blood-boilingly angering to me that it is not a knife-wielding attacker that is dehumanised in a catastrophe like this, it is the innocent. It is the victim. *They* are the evidence; *they* are the ones whose bodies are put back together so that their family can see them and supposedly not be traumatised. Polly had asked the detectives time and time again as to why they thought Jamie had been stabbed. They said in these kinds of cases, the reasonings behind attacks such as Jamie's can really vary. They say *Jamie's attack*, *Jamie's murde*r, as though they belong to him, like it's something that he chose. Their ignorance and tactlessness made me want to scream. The detectives said to Polly that from what the eyewitnesses have all said, the accused appeared to be jealous of Jamie, and he resented his popularity. He was at the bar alone; he was desperate for a reaction. He was attention seeking; he leered at Rachel, and he tried to put his hands on her chest, knowing Jamie would intervene. When Jamie confronted the accused, he ended up getting stabbed. Multiple times. Polly sickeningly appeared to want to know every last detail; a blow-by-blow account of each and every wound. She said she wanted to understand why the killer had done such a thing, she had so many unanswered questions. I thought this said it all really. All Polly had done since we had got to the mortuary, was jabber on non-stop about the killer. I just wanted to see my boy. In some respects, I wish I hadn't. The young man lying on that mortuary slab didn't look like Jamie. He didn't look like my boy; bubbly and bold and brilliant. He looked murdered. He looked like a corpse.

I had screamed and screamed and screamed. Polly steered me out of the room; she was crying too. She frog-marched me to the car, she tried hard to console me but the bottom line was that I had seen the unseeable: my baby boy, his murdered body before me.

Polly had been watching me like a hawk since then. I'd noticed that she had removed all of the medicines from the medicine cabinet. She followed me around everywhere now; trailing after me like Greyfriars gone wrong.

She'd had the gall to stand there until I got out of the bath. Polly and I had shared a bedroom when we were young girls and I never dressed and undressed openly in front of her. I would have always turned away, modestly and primly, hating the thought of being seen by her looking indecent. I'd wrapped myself quickly in my towel and exploded at Polly. I told her I had had just about enough of her breathing down my neck all of the time; constantly feeling monitored, and surveyed. I was so seething, that I think she knew she probably needed to get out of my way, pronto.

I sat in my bedroom, alone with my thoughts. Thoughts of Jamie. The horrible thought of him at the mortuary plagued me. It seeped its way into all of the good memories; it was taking over. There was a sense of that thought stealing all of the amazing memories created with Jamie; it was as though who he had been and the life that he had led, was starting to slip further and further away. It was like having sand slipping through my fingers. What I couldn't seem to let go of, no matter how hard I tried, was how he had looked, lying there. Seeing his murdered body, it had prompted my mind to feel violated in the most despicable way, comprehensible. I mentally felt attacked and agonised; my head pulsed constantly with the turmoil. It was getting too much. It was as though I was immersed in what those last moments must have been like for Jamie. I tried desperately hard not to think about it, but I couldn't seem to think of anything else. I leaned down beneath my bed and pulled out a bottle of wine. I unscrewed the lid and glugged urgently. I needed a distraction; I needed something else to focus on, even if it was just for a few minutes.

Polly opened the door tentatively. She looked pained as she registered the wine.

"Is that a good idea?" she quizzed patronisingly.

My lip curled at the sound of her voice. I didn't acknowledge her. *How dare she stand in my home and try and lecture me!* She'd been known as the family lush since the beginning of time, so if she thought she could be a condescending mare to me in my own home, she could whistle! What was she even *doing* here anyway? When was she going to push off home?

Polly came right into the room and sat down at the edge of the bed. She looked at me as though I was a scared, snappy dog that she really hoped wasn't going to bite her.

"I really don't want to annoy you, Susanna. I knew you needed space earlier so I thought I'd keep to myself for a while, stay downstairs so you could be on your own."

She rubbed her temple.

"I'm just so worried about you."

I carried on drinking. The noise sounded unpleasant even to my own ears, but I kept on steadily drinking.

Polly sighed heavily.

"Come on, Susanna, drinking alone at all hours is always a recipe for disaster."

I ignored her. I hoped she'd take the hint that I didn't want to talk to her, but she still remained. I couldn't help but interpret her stubbornness as spite.

"Well, if you can't beat them, join them. Give us a sip then," she said with a sigh. I handed her the bottle silently. She took a quick sip.

"I remember when we were teenagers and Mum used to go spare when she'd come up and see us drinking in our bedroom on a Saturday night."

She shook her head, smiling.

"Looking back, poor old Mum must have been at her wit's end with me. I thought I was so cool. Acting like a wild child the minute I hit fourteen when really, I should have just put my head down, and stayed on the straight and narrow. Caused her less aggro."

She looked at me expectantly, as though she was assuming, I would be in a rush to reassure her. I stared at her reproachfully.

"Well, you always were selfish," I said pointedly. "Thinking of anyone else's feelings was never your forte."

Polly took another gulp of wine; it felt as though she was building up to something.

"I was so jealous of you when were younger, Susanna. You had the looks, all those boys dropping at your feet, whereas you never let the attention go straight to your head. You just wanted to play wifey with Tom. I always had to be all-singing, all-dancing to even be noticed."

I looked at her incredulously.

"I'm astonished that even you could be so self-absorbed at a time like this!"

I took a great big glug of wine.

"I know you like playing the victim, acting like you were all hard-done-by once upon a time. But let's be honest here, Polly. You were always an attention-seeking, mollycoddled little madam that was pandered to far too much! You couldn't BEAR to see anybody that wasn't you getting so much as a scrap of happiness."

Polly gulped; she knew where I was heading with this. She knew what elephant in the room I was going to release from its enclosure.

"You couldn't stand to see how amazing things were between Tom and I! You did nothing but nit-pick and criticise, you were so desperate to talk me out of staying with him. But of course, that's because you were desperate to get your paws on him yourself. Well, you tried to. You made a pass at him the day after I'd told you I was pregnant with Jamie because you are a malicious, jaded little bitch!"

Polly regarded me, she had the grace to look briefly ashamed.

"I was in a really bad place then, Susanna, you know that. I was jealous, I felt completely left on the shelf. You were my little sister and you'd overtaken me, as far as I was concerned. I can only apologise for being a desperate cow then, but what good is going to come of raking over all of that now? The past is the past, I thought all of that was water under the bridge now."

I glared at her.

Polly patted my hand.

"I know we've had our differences in the past, but you know you can always talk to me about anything."

I yanked my hand away, as though she'd poured toxic waste all over me. She looked stricken by my response.

"Why the *fuck* would I talk to you?" I barked.

"We've never been close, ever. We were never exactly as thick as thieves were we? Putting the world to rights over the kitchen table?"

I laughed, the sound escaping me, bitter and brittle.

"We weren't even close as *kids.* How sad is that- especially with it just being the two of us!"

Polly was evidently strained, she clearly didn't want to go there.

"Susanna, you're over-tired, you're stressed, and you're grieving. Why don't you get an early night and we can talk in the morning?"

I was livid.

"Why don't you fuck off home and not come back in the morning? Oh wait, that would be too bloody real, too genuine."

I had another drink, I was gathering momentum.

"You don't hang around here, wrapping me up in cotton wool because you CARE. It's all about 'Keeping up Appearances' with you. What's going to look good, what would people expect of Polly fucking Pocket? Do you not think I see you, talking to the neighbours out there, going on like you're bloody Mother Theresa?"

I rolled my eyes, Polly wasn't even looking at me. She stared at her lap fixated, as I let off steam.

"It's ironic that it takes my son being MURDERED for you to start acting like a sister. You've lived around the corner for fifteen years and you never popped around to see me until you got the call to say that MY BOY…"

"My nephew," Polly had the cheek to whisper.

I wanted to slap her.

"MY CHILD IS DEAD!" I boomed.

Polly began to cry.

I was steely.

"From day dot, Polly, you made it clear that you never wanted kids. You always made it plain that runny noses, bath-times, spaghetti-fucking hoops weren't for you. You don't have children so you will NEVER understand what this feels like. You will never understand how I PHYSICALLY ACHE because I want my son back so much! You will never feel suffocated by merciless grief. You will never feel like the walls are just closing on you!"

Polly sobbed, she claimed she did understand as she took my dad's death so badly. She knew how awful grief was. This, to me, was laughable.

"That was completely different! It was a shame, it was sad! But there was still a light at the end of the tunnel. I could still see that the world kept on turning. Whereas this…"

I pointed shakily.

"THIS is on a completely different scale. I feel like I'm just stuck, DROWNING and I weirdly don't want to be brought up for air because I know I'm not going to be brought back to my old life! I'm sick of living in this misery…my…"

My voice cracked.

"Reality."

Polly attempted to hug me; she mumbled how she so wanted to take all of this away from me. I couldn't stand her touching me. I hated the way that she always had to constantly invade my personal space. I shoved her. Hard. She fell off the bed to the floor and narrowly missed hitting her head on the floor. She looked winded, but she rose slowly to her feet and backed towards the door.

"I'll give you some space, Susanna," she said sombrely.

Then

Someone pounded at the front door; the noise was deafening. I stayed on the floor; I physically felt paralysed. It was as if someone was pressing down hard on my chest. I felt suffocated, strangled. It was as though there was no *air.*

"Susanna, open the door!" Polly cried.

"Please open the door, let me in!"

Adam rushed down the stairs, hurriedly wiping his face roughly with the back of his sleeve. He manoeuvred his way around me and made for the door. He turned to me briefly, his face tilted to one side, pretending to look concerned.

"Mum, we need to open the door to her. We need our family around us."

It felt as though he'd kicked me. Sensing my rising anger, he quickly turned and opened the door. Polly hurtled in from the doorstep; turbulent and terrifying. Her make-up was smeared; her hair wild and dishevelled, as though she'd been pulling at it. She used to pull her hair sometimes when she was a little girl, having a temper tantrum. It used to really panic my parents; they feared she had a psychiatric problem of some sort. She didn't. She was just an egotistical shrew that wanted constant adulation and gratification.

Polly flew into Adam; embracing him tightly.

"Oh my God, Adam, you poor little mite. I just don't know what to say. I thought that I was in a nightmare when you said that our J…"

She gulped; her nose was running very badly. It was starting to dribble down to her lip. Adam looked fleetingly nauseated before swiftly handing her a tissue, which she gratefully received. After quickly wiping her nose, she tried to compose herself enough to talk.

"I couldn't *believe* it when you said our J had been STABBED."

She uttered the last word with the exaggeration and intonation, that children secretly utter swear words that they've heard, to their friends.

Polly rubbed the back of her head, bewildered.

“I mean, STABBED? How did this even happen, stabbing happens between rival gangs. Our J wasn’t caught up in anything like that.”

She was starting to sound more and more hysterical.

“None of this makes any sense.”

For the first time since she’d arrived, she actually looked at me, withered on the floor. Her eyes fleetingly filled with tears. She wasn’t going to hug me, we didn’t hug, it wasn’t our thing. We’d always laughed and joked and claimed it was because we were just too British. That wasn’t it at all, we just had never really had the sort of relationship where we would actually show affection to one another. Polly looked as though she was at a loss as to what to say or do. She settled eventually upon flying her hand up to our mouth as she stood there looming above me; tears streaming down her face.

“Susanna, I wish I knew what to say. This is, this is just…”

She waved her hand about, searching for the right word.

“This PAIN, it’s just…”

I stared at her levelly. She squirmed slightly under my gaze.

“This pain is just like being stabbed,” I uttered, with a subdued sense of certainty.

Polly’s mouth gaped open like a post box; her face as red as a lobster’s. Adam looked vaguely alarmed before pulling her into him. Polly clung to him desperately; she sprung at him so suddenly, it looked as though they’d both topple over. Polly always underestimated how small Adam was and he was as light as a feather too. Ironically though, Adam, who normally had abysmal posture, was standing as tall as a tree; his posture perfect. It was as though this news had elevated him; both metaphorically and literally. I wanted to scream and scream but I couldn’t bear the thought of either of them touching me; being near me. Adam looked as though he was contemplating hugging me at one point. I found myself physically convulsing at this effort. I recoiled to such an extent that even Polly appeared to get the message.

She hugged Adam instead; the pair resembling two spoons. They were a handful of steps away from me but I felt as though they were in a separate entity entirely. It was like being on a platform at a train station; alone with your thoughts scrambling around your mind as you looked across at the other people waiting too. I stared at Adam and Polly. You would have expected us to all be hanging on to each other, wailing and weeping. But I couldn’t bear to bring myself to collapse against them, to perceive them as my anchors. Because they weren't. They never had been. They sure as hell, never would be. I looked at them, from my crumpled crevices on the floor. I surveyed Polly and Adam, talking soothingly to each other as they sniffled and snuffled. For them, it was abundant that their worlds had stopped, halted temporarily. My world hadn't stopped. It had ended.

Now

I sloped downstairs, my bones feeling like weights. I physically felt impaired since Jamie's death. It was as though I was only capable of shuffling these days. I frequently felt as though I was in slow motion. It was as though everything had changed. It was like being suddenly stripped of a world of colour, dynamicity and hope. Everything was endlessly dull and bleak now; it was impossible to feel any sense of optimism. I'd once read intensely about grief. It had been years ago, not long after my dad's death. I had actually been really anxious about Polly; she didn't seem to be coping with the loss at all. She cried all the time and she fell into an undeniable state of depression. I had found my father's death to be a sad and indeed confusing time. He had had lung cancer for three years and he was in significant pain, in the days leading up to his death. I had done my very best to make him feel as comfortable as possible and I made a point of constantly keeping the focus on my dad at all times. Polly didn't spend much time with him at all in the run-up to his death. She sat downstairs and gorged like there was no tomorrow on all the sandwiches and sausage rolls that my mum seemed to forever be making. My Mum had always been a homemaker and her go-to when stressed, was to cook and bake as if her life depended on it. She, too, didn't spend an awful lot of time with my dad in the period before his death. My mum had always adopted a *stiff upper lip,* approach to grief. That was just her way. I knew that my mum had been knocked sideways by my dad's terminal diagnosis. It had looked as though he was getting better; he seemed to be out of the woods, for the most part. My mum was mystified at how we could go from having hope to such a morose sense of finality in a matter of minutes. The doom and dread that she experienced were profound, I really do think it left her feeling shattered.

I remembered the last conversation I had with my dad. I'd been downstairs trying to pose as a shoulder to cry on for Polly. She sat, drinking her 100th cup of tea of the afternoon, spraying the crumbs of her Madeira slice as she said over and over again that it just wasn't fair; she couldn't believe that this was happening to her. She needed her dad; she felt robbed as though valuable time had been snatched from her. I remembered silently screaming inside my head that it appeared to be rather ironic that she was already starting to talk about our dad in the past tense despite the fact that he was still alive and upstairs. It may well be a good idea to go up and to spend some time with him whilst she still could as opposed to sitting on the sofa all day, stuffing her face. I tried to coax her into coming up with me to talk with my dad but she insisted that she was like a *bucket of water,* and it would be too much for her. It was best that I went and dealt with him. I had always been able to keep it together so much better. I had felt silently resentful as I made my way upstairs; it was tiring always having to be the capable, contained one that kept everything in order.

I remembered the shock of seeing my dad lying in his bed, suddenly so s*mall*. I remembered my dad as being tall and strong, he'd been my hero as a child. Seeing him so fragile and weak had nearly reduced me to tears. I'll never forget the way that he insisted that I wiped those tears away pronto, before urging me to not waste precious time wallowing over his death. He had reassured me that he'd had a good run of it. He'd had a great life and he could honestly say that at the end, he had no regrets. He had urged me to not feel guilty for getting out there and for living my life, as after all, it's natural that little by little we let go of loss, but never of love. He told me that I was to concentrate on the boys and that they were my future, they would guide me through the grief. He'd told me that grief to him had always felt so like fear and things would stop being so scary when I embraced living again; when I decided to grab the bull by the horns and to enjoy life once more. He reminded me that I didn't fall apart after Tom's death. I'd been able to get my priorities straight and realise that the best way I could honour him would be by pouring all of my focus and love into our boy. I remembered how touched I was that my dad was at such pains to share his advice on grief for me, even though it must have hurt him so terribly to have such a painful conversation with his child. Plus, he'd never been a big talker at all. My mum had been the chatterer; constantly wittering and twittering. My dad had always sat on his armchair, listening intently and chipping in with the occasional, "Yes, dear", "No, dear", and, "I suppose." But because my dad had always been a man of few words, the words he did utter always seemed to carry such extra meaning. They carried far more weight and vitality than the average persons.

I held on to his words for such a long time. I had felt sad when my dad died, it was strange to know that I couldn't pop around and have a cup of tea with both him *and* Mum anymore. I had had a lifetime of happy memories with him and it did sting that he wasn't around anymore, he was the epitome of a *good egg*. But it was bearable. I had been so lucky; I'd had a great father and a whole host of wonderful memories had been created that I could look back on and smile at. I focused on the good, I focused on the *love* as he had advised me to do so and in my experience, he was right. I did learn to let go of the loss and I was able to focus on the love. I remembered talking with Jamie when he was a teenager about this and was really surprised by what he'd said to me. He emphasised that we shouldn't cry because it was over, we should smile because it had happened. I was shocked at the profoundness and splendour of this statement and praised Jamie on his beautiful outlook. I had asked him how he had thought of such a beautiful statement that just seemed to encapsulate grief perfectly. He had shrugged, before admitting with a laugh. "As much as I would love to take credit for that quote, I'm afraid that would be a big whopper of a lie. No, I got it from someone very wise indeed. Dr Seuss, to be exact!"

I think I've always found it fascinating how grief is something that affects us all, at some point or another but it's strange that so many people are conditioned to believe that we have to lead two lives: one where we pretend to other people that everything is okay and that we're starting to muddle on. The other life we lead is behind closed doors; where we find ourselves inwardly screaming because it's all so unfair and we can't believe that this is happening to us, because this wasn't how it was supposed to be. This feeling is felt intensely on an inward basis over a deeply unhappy period. Then it starts to get easier, and it eventually gets to a stage, where the two lives we portray start to not resemble two separate entities, we're able to *"fake it until we make it"* if you will until the two lives start to concord into one. The loss hasn't changed but it becomes easier to put one foot in front of the other. We can begin to dip our toes back into the ocean of life once more and remind ourselves that it's not all filled with troubled waters.

But what happens when it goes horribly wrong: when a death happens that goes against the grain of the Circle of Life? How can life be so cruel to make a mother outlive her child? To have to live in a world devoid of meaning and purpose? My existence used to be one of screaming colours. Jamie was the canvas of my existence. He was the reason that the other bereavements I had had were survivable; he was my focus, my reason for waking up in the morning. Without him, life can only be classed as an abyss, bottomless and barbaric, mercilessly tormenting.

I made my way down the stairs. I could hear Polly in the kitchen; she was talking to someone on the phone. She was none the wiser to my presence and she obliviously dug quite the hole for herself.

"Oh, my goodness, I know. It's awful. I'm doing my best for her, but it's difficult to know what to say and what to do. I have to scrape her off the floor most days. She's not washing, she's not got any motivation to do anything at the minute."

Polly was sizzling bacon on the pan.

"She is just so lost; so hopeless. I suppose I'm trying to remember that it's my job to get her out of this, although heaven help me, it's certainly an uphill battle at the mo. After all, I've dropped everything to be here for her indefinitely and she's not giving me so much as an inch. I'm just so drained. It really does take it out of you caring for someone so miserable. I am worried that I'm not expressing my grief properly too. I don't want to end up paying the price later for rushing around like a headless chicken, looking after everyone else. Yeah, I know. I know. I'll try and look after number one more, I will. Charity starts at home, after all."

I stalked into the room. She spun around, thrown. She looked alarmed; she was clearly trying to gauge how much I'd heard. She wrapped up her call and smiled her sickly sweet grin at me. She rapidly buttered a roll and plopped the bacon in.

"Morning, Susana," she trilled, like a vindictive bird.

She glanced at the clock; it was 11:50 am.

"Well, barely!"

I glowered at her. She looked nervous before handing me over the bacon roll.

"Here, tuck into this. I know that bacon sandwiches are your favourites!"

I regarded it with disgust before striding out of the room, deftly throwing the bacon sandwich into the bin before leaving. Polly looked irked.

"For God's sake, Susanna, why did you do that? Will you look at me? I'm talking to you, for crying out loud."

I went upstairs, ignoring her.

I hated her.

Then

I woke up, my sheets were a tangled mess. I had a crick in my neck. I sat up, rubbing at the back of my neck. I know it's a common expression but it's bizarre to me that it's actually so easy to forget how irritating it is to have an actual pain in the neck. I sat up, my head was throbbing too. Not exactly the best start to the day.

Suddenly, I felt anguish bestow upon me, sinister angst enveloping my features, engulfing my heart and mind. How on earth could I be stupid enough to sit there thinking about a sore neck and head when Jamie was…

No, he couldn't be. It was some sort of mistake; some kind of horrible mistake. Jamie would be in his room on the other side of the landing. He'd be lying in his bed; he'd moan when I'd open the door, he wouldn't be able to fathom why I'd burst into the room at ridiculous o'clock. He'd be puzzled when I'd tell him that I just wanted to see him as I'd had the most horrific nightmare and he had been *murdered* and despite the fact that it wasn't reality, it just felt so real; so raw. I'd tell him that a police officer had come around late last night. He had confirmed what Max had told me earlier. He had told me that he was sorry for my loss. Jamie would lean over; he'd give me a big hug and assure me that he wasn't going anywhere. He'd joke teasingly that there were still heaps of things he had to do yet, he hadn't had two wives and four children and he'd not yet scooped the big lottery win. Then I'd call myself a daft idiot for attaching too much credence to a blooming nightmare and I'd go down and prepare some breakfast for him and I. Bacon and eggs; a Full English if there was enough in the fridge. I really needed to do a Big Shop, we'd be having beans on toast for the next few days if I didn't get to the supermarket, pronto.

I rushed across the landing; I raced like my life depended on it. I pulled Jamie's bedroom door open…his room was empty. I knew that straight away, of course, I did, but I decided to be thorough. I double-checked, I pulled back his duvet despite the fact that I knew he wasn't minute enough to be hiding beneath that; Jamie's feet always poked out comically at the end of the bed because he was so tall. I knew I was being ridiculous but I didn't care. I peered beneath the bed; I looked in his wardrobe in case he happened to be crouching in there, biding his time before leaping out at me, hooting with laughter. But desperate people keep trying even when they privately know that the situation isn't going to change. I wildly searched Jamie's room, yearning for him to be there somewhere. I tried to will him into the room. I would turn around and he'd be standing there, a cup of coffee in hand; telling me with an apologetic smile that he'd finished off the last of the bread but he'd go to the corner shop later, buy us another loaf or two. I f*elt* someone standing behind me, and I beamed. I'd longed for him so much, that I'd been able to materialise him.

I spun around. It wasn't Jamie. It was Adam.

He stood there, in his pea-green pyjamas. His hair was mussed-up as though he'd spent much of the night tossing and turning. He was so pale that he looked luminous. He alarmingly resembled one of those cheap white glow sticks that you get at festivals and kid's discos. I felt revolted at the sight of him. I turned away, I didn't want to look at him. If I was wasting my time looking at him, I wasn't wishing Jamie back. I tried to blot Adam out, I needed to focus. I wasn't going to allow *him* to deter me. I suddenly heard the wardrobe open and shut. I shot around, perplexed. Adam had reached into *Jamie's* wardrobe, he had pulled on *Jamie's* football shirt. He stroked it; his ghoulish fingers tracing the shirt, up and down, up and down. It was as though he was trying to scrape Jamie off his own belongings. He was hell-bent on trying to corrupt Jamie's belongings, to taint his room, his space. I felt myself shaking with rage.

He looked at me; the faintest glimmer of a smirk was flashed at me.

"I just wanted to feel *close* to him. It's not even been twenty-four hours yet, but it already feels like it's been years."

He outstretched his arms; initiating an embrace.

"Come here, Mum. You look so helpless, so afraid. You were always looking after me. Let me take care of you, for once."

I watched him wearing Jamie's shirt. I wanted to rip it off him. But I didn't want to risk tearing it; Jamie adored that shirt. I vowed that I'd wash it the second he took it off. I'd prise it off him if I really had to. Then I'd fumigate it, I would make sure that there was no trace of a single *pore* of Adam left on Jamie's shirt.

Adam sniffed.

"It's strange. It sort of feels like I'm hugging him. This still smells of Jamie."

Oh, God. Suddenly, I felt weak. If I washed Jamie's shirt, I'd be removing Adam's odour, sure, but I'd also be removing any traces of Jamie. The football shirt would smell of washing powder, it would no longer smell of Jamie. Adam was leaning into the wardrobe again. He was rubbing Jamie's jumper sleeves to his face, breathing in his scent. I couldn't stand it anymore. I wrenched his gnarled fingers away from Jamie's clothes and shoved him out of the room. A combination of rage and adrenaline meant that I practically threw him out on to the landing. Adam looked blindsided.

"Don't you *dare* go into Jamie's room again, you grotesque little creep!" I snarled.

Adam looked taken aback.

"If you so much as think about going into Jamie's room again, you really will be at the end of my wrath. You vile little snake," I spat.

"Dear, dear, dear," I heard someone say.

I turned to see Polly coming up the stairs slowly, as she balanced a tray laden with a cup of tea so milky it could only be described as chalk-white; a glass of watery orange juice and a bacon sandwich.

"I think she's only being so snappy because she's hungry. Don't look so woe begone, Adam," Polly said with infuriating cheeriness. She was acting as though I was a peckish puppy being a pain because I'd not yet had my kibble, as opposed to a grief-stricken Mum, whose child had just been *murdered.* I felt it; that jolt, that painful piercing sensation every time I thought or heard that word. That *stab*.

Polly tried to briskly encourage me to go back to bed; to have my breakfast there as if it was some kind of special treat.

"Come on, Susanna, you love bacon sandwiches," she simpered.

I looked at the food. I looked at *her* and *him*. I dissolved into tears.

Now

I sat on the living room floor, surrounded by photos of Jamie from babyhood to adulthood. I couldn't be bothered to shower, it seemed like such an effort. The thought of the whole rigmarole of undressing and washing and dressing just seemed like far too tall an order; completely and utterly pointless. I hadn't bathed for a few days either as Polly now insisted on the bathroom door being ajar when I was in there having a bath. I was surprised that she let me go to the toilet unaccompanied. I wouldn't rule out her sitting on the edge of the bath when I was on the loo. It was so violating, so encroaching. I didn't think it was too great an ask to expect some privacy for basic things like toileting and bathing. I wondered how Polly would feel if she couldn't so much as have a soak anymore without me hovering, watching her every move. "The *Every Step You Take*," song came into my head. It escaped me as to who sang it. It dawned on me: the Police. I couldn't hear the word "Police" without thinking of the "Investigation". This inevitably made me think of what had happened to Jamie; it made me think of seeing him dead on that slab. It frightened me that that memory seemed to have an overruling effect in that it was the memory that dominated my mind. I tried desperately hard to think of all the good memories but I couldn't run away from how he'd looked, how he didn't look like my Jamie. That monster had stripped me of that. That murderer had made sure that the sight I saw was so abominably distressing that it seemed to cloud over Jamie and all he was. I couldn't lose sight of that. I needed to remember, remember, remember.

I looked at Jamie as a young baby; undeniably perfect. I looked at him as a toddler and saw him playing with his favourite toy, a yellow duck called Dennis. He had adored that toy; he constantly went adventuring with him around the garden, toddling around on his chubby little legs. I remembered him screaming fit to burst anytime I dared try and peel Dennis from his clasp so that he could have a spin in the washing machine. Due to all the adventures he went on, Dennis did start to smell rather questionable indeed. Jamie didn't play with him as much when he got to school age. From then on out, Dennis resided beneath his bed. Jamie had cleared out lots of his old cuddly toys when he'd got to about sixteen, he said he didn't need them anymore. It made sense to donate them to charity, then they could be played with again by children as opposed to gathering dust beneath his bed. He'd laughed, he'd joked how he felt like Andy from "*Toy Story*." He had played all these miniature games with all of the toys nostalgically before placing them with care into a great big box, ready to be taken to the hospice shop. He'd paused wistfully when he reached Dennis; he'd hesitated before putting him sadly into the box with the rest of the toys. He'd looked relieved when I'd told him that I thought that he ought to keep at least one special childhood toy, it seemed a shame to give away all of them. Dennis from there on out lived at the bottom of Jamie's wardrobe, where he'd see him every day, as opposed to being tucked out of sight beneath his bed, shrouded in the dark. I vowed to find Dennis later, to rub my cheek against his yellow matted fur. It might help me to feel a little closer to Jamie; it physically hurt that he was starting to feel slightly distant already. I couldn't bear it. That was why I had to keep remembering him. I had to remember the sound of his laugh, the warmth of his smile, the heartiness and cheer with which he spoke with. Because if I couldn't bring Jamie to life in my head alone; the way he had been, the way that he was, it was as though I had had ever since fibre of him snatched from me. I meticulously scanned each and every photograph. I couldn't be interrupted; I had to ignore every single disturbance if I wanted to succeed.

Polly came into the room; holding a cup of tea as usual. She registered me. She appeared genuinely shocked. I knew I looked terrible. I tended to avoid the mirror at all costs, but sometimes I caught a glimpse of myself in the big mirror in the living room when I went in to look through photographs of Jamie. I looked dishevelled; my hair resembled a bird's nest, for starters. I had scraped my hair back into a bun a couple of days ago and hadn't redone it since. It had escaped the confines of its hair band for the most part and it sat in greasy clumps around my head. I knew that it needed washing very badly. I had previously washed my hair every single morning and now it had practically been a fortnight since I'd even bothered to brush it. Or had it been longer than a fortnight? Time didn't seem to have any meaning now. Sometimes I'd be sitting at the kitchen table listening to Polly witter on, as she made me ham-and-cheese sandwiches, desperate to feed me up. Polly had bitterly remarked that I appeared to just be wasting away whilst she appeared to be piling on the pounds, by simply thinking about a packet of crisps. These grumbles and groans appeared to be never-ending. I often felt that hours must have passed, when usually it only manifested to be five minutes or so that had elapsed. Sometimes I sat on the living room floor, looking at photos of Jamie and assumed that I'd only been there for about half an hour or so. Then I'd peer at the clock and discover that I'd actually been there for the best part of five hours. Time just doesn't seem to bear any significance to me anymore.

I noticed Polly looking at my murky-grey tracksuit bottoms. I'd had them for donkey's years. I'd formerly only used them in the past for a day spent doing housework. I lived in them now; they were quick and easy and the thought of wearing any item of clothing other than them was unthinkable. I shrieked if Polly ever attempted to urge me to take them off so that she could give them a wash. She'd claim that she'd give them back to me straight away. She conceded that even I must have been able to see that they were in dire need of a freshen up. Polly infuriated me to such an extent that I found I had to resist every instinct to not groan whenever she walked into the room. My top was an old purple thing; baggy and comfy. I'd last worn it when I was pregnant with Jamie. I didn't want to take that off, not ever.

Polly put the cup of tea down on the mantelpiece. She attempted to sit down beside me but she couldn't bend too much in her jeans. Polly insisted upon never getting jeans that fitted her properly. She'd never buy the correct size for herself, she would always insist that she'd lose the timber, that the smaller size would motivate her to lose weight. She never did, which meant that most of the time she went around in jeans that she could barely breathe or indeed walk in. I watched her warily as she struggled to sit up on her knees beside me. She looked at the photos; she knew better than to attempt to touch any. Polly wound an arm around my shoulders. I think she wanted us to have a *moment*. She could whistle, I knew that she just wanted me to weep on her shoulder and thank her for being so amazing, for being my rock. Polly would then tell this story to anyone who was mad enough to be prepared to listen and they'd praise her for being such a remarkable sister, she sought to be hailed as an inspiration. The thought of this mortifying scene was enough to make me feel as though I could well need a bucket passed my way.

Polly sensed that she wasn't getting anywhere and staggered to her feet, with a sigh.

“Adam’s coming back early from school today, Susanna, he’s not staying on at the library to do his homework. I thought we could all go out to the kitchen, have a spot of tea together. You always loved afternoon teas. I think it would be nice for us to spend some proper time together. I know that we see each other every day, but it doesn’t actually feel that we *talk,* a great deal. Not properly, it just feels like we all sort of tip-toe around each other.”

This is a thinly veiled dig – she didn’t think that we tiptoed around each other. She seemed to be under the impression that she and Adam tiptoed around me. I sniffed. I couldn’t care less what the likes of them thought anyway. I’d never asked them to keep me under house arrest; to pose as my two jailors. I couldn’t stand having to share the same space as either of them. I wished that they would both just *go.*

I heard the key in the front door. Seconds later, Adam slinked into the room.

“Adam, you’re back!” Polly announced loudly as though I was indeed blind and deaf.

“Terrific, just in time for tea. I’ve made the scones and some cake. A nice Vicky sponge, which I know we all like.”

I felt like I’d been slapped.

“Don’t call it a Vicky sponge,” I said through gritted teeth.

Polly looked bemused.

“Why ever not, Susanna?” she asked, gallingly self-righteous.

“Because that’s what Jamie called it!” I snapped.

“That was his phrase, not yours. Don’t ever call it that again.”

Polly was clearly rattled. She took a shuddery breath, as though steadying herself. Adam went up to her; gave her shoulder a squeeze. She seemed to be grateful for the solidarity. Two abysmal allies together. Them against me.

Adam smiled at me; the gesture was disturbing.

“I’ve got some nice biscuits too, Mum. I picked them up on the way home from school. Ginger ones, I know that they’re your favourite.”

Polly grinned.

“Thanks, Adam,” she chirped.

“I’ll set the tea all out then. You tell your Mum all about your day. I’m sure she’d love to hear about it. I’ll call you when it’s ready.”

Adam came and sat down on the floor. I didn’t acknowledge his presence. I needed to focus on Jamie, on the masses of smiling Jamie’s all around me.

"I had an okay day today, Mum. I found out that I got into Imperial today. It was sad, given that Jamie isn't here to tell. He knew that was where I had my heart set on. Oxford and Cambridge are great if you want that kind of thing, but I think the pressure would have just been too much. I've got to be true to myself too, that's what Jamie would have wanted."

I ignored him, although I could feel anger starting to bubble in the pit of my stomach.

"Come on, you pair!" Polly babbled. She had suddenly appeared again and was evidently wanting to diffuse the situation. She knew I was edging closer towards tipping point.

"We've run out of sugar for the tea, I'll just have to go without. Ho hum, I can go to the co-op tomorrow and grab some. You could come with me, Susanna. Get some fresh air, get out of the house."

I blanked her.

Adam looked at all of the photographs. It was as though he was trying to poison them. I couldn't stand someone as hateful as him even being able to look at someone as glorious as Jamie. I felt my blood boil.

"How long have you been looking at all of these?" he asked.

I didn't utter a response.

Adam peered at an old holiday snap, of Jamie larking around on the beach.

"Do you remember that holiday to Alicante? The hotel manager's daughter falling head over heels in love with Jamie? Do you remember how she was begging him to stay out there, to do some bar work at the hotel so they could stay together, as she couldn't bear the thought of him returning to England?"

He laughed; the sound was insincere.

"Raquel, her name was. Jamie got teased mercilessly when he returned home and introduced his next girlfriend to everybody as Rachel."

I steadily ignored him – how dare he talk about Jamie? He didn't even deserve to have his name pass his loathsome lips.

"I always remember Jamie saying to Max that before he left Alicante, Raquel turned around and told him that life without him was just going to be miserable."

He stared down at the photo, his eyes calculated and cold.

"I know exactly what she means."

He squeezed out a crocodile tear or so. I felt deep-rooted disgust, I couldn't stomach his presence for much longer at all. Polly came over to him, I heard a ripping noise as she bent over so suddenly in her ridiculous jeans to hug him.

She looked at me disapprovingly over his shoulder. She wanted me to comfort him, to placate him. No chance. I ignored both of them. I carried on with my task.

"Jamie was amazing," Adam said suddenly.

His tone was goading.

"He was an exceptional person."

He picked up a photograph of Jamie, a recent one, taken on his 21st. That was the final straw – that python had pushed me too far!

"Put. That. Down!" I snarled, the words escaping me in a sense of breathless contempt.

Adam looked startled. Polly looked strained.

I rose to my feet and Polly glanced at me fretfully, as though I was a wild animal on the loose.

"Put that down," I repeated vehemently to Adam.

He dropped the photograph to the floor. It curled slightly at the edge; it was going to be dog-eared permanently now because of that little freak!

"Don't you ever touch a photograph of MY SON!" I screeched.

Adam looked aghast.

"He was my brother, Mum! I need to remember him too!"

This comment was so incensing that I felt as though I could burst.

"He was your brother when it suited! You were so TOXIC and you'd watch him wasting all of his energy as he tried to constantly cheer you up 24/7!"

Adam sobbed; Polly's mouth was gaping open, as though she was ready to catch a family of flies.

"Please don't take everything out on me, Mum," Adam pleaded, his eyes shining with callousness.

"He was worth TEN of you. He was kind, compassionate, considerate – everything that you will never, ever be!"

I stepped toward him. He leapt backwards as though I was armed.

"I can only imagine how much you're loving walking around these streets at the moment. Poor billy-no-mates, Adam lapping up all of the attention. Only a foul little freak like you would get a kick out of your ADORED brother being murdered."

Adam shook his head slowly; looking at Polly.

"That's really unfair, Mum," he said, as he rubbed his face with his hands.

"No, what's unfair is the fact that my gorgeous J is dead!" I bellowed.

Polly tried to take my hand.

"Susanna, we are all in the same boat! This is awful for everybody. You don't need to make matters even worse by being horrid to Adam and I, who are only trying to help you!"

She looked tearful.

"You need to stop pushing us away, Susanna. I don't mind if it makes you feel better treating me like dirt every once in a while, but you need to stop lashing out at Adam. He's your son!"

I glared at them both.

"Jamie was my son," I hissed.

Adam stared at me, cutting and conspiring.

"Don't ever touch photos of my son again!" I spat.

I sat back on the floor, trying to concentrate on Jamie once more. Polly led Adam out of the room. I let out a breath; I despised them both.

Then

I had always been a house-proud person. Before Jamie died, I used to be up every morning at the crack of dawn, vacuuming the house like a trojan before getting showered and dressed for work. I always used to think that it stood me in good stead for the day. I'd kick-started my day with something proactive; positive. I couldn't abide a messy house. I'd always been particular in that regard, right from being a child. Since Jamie's death, I'd not attempted to do any housework. It suddenly seemed such a futile and feckless task. I had bigger fish to fry; I needed to think about Jamie and look through all of his photographs. You would have assumed that Polly would have tried to keep herself busy by making sure that the place was as ship-shape as what it could be, on the cleanliness front, but that would have been too useful of course. Too practical. Instead, she occupied herself by making incessant cups of tea for her and I. She sat transfixed in the kitchen for most of the morning as she watched breakfast television. She probably viewed this as her, *time for herself,* because I rarely came downstairs before noon these days. From the afternoon onwards, she followed me around the house all day, giving me cups of tea that I hadn't asked for and saying stupid things like, "Do you think it might be an idea to put on a little make-up today, Susanna? It might make you feel more of a *woman*, again. I know I always look like *death* before I put my face on." I couldn't fathom why she insisted upon posing as my stalker, day in and day out. I'd never asked her to come, I'd never asked her to move in. She just *did*. I wasn't even consulted, despite the fact that it was my house. She had even hinted that she'd quite like to sleep in Jamie's room, as it was ever so cramped in the box room. The nerve of her! I hoped she'd get rickets from being crammed into the minuscule room and then she'd have to hobble on home to her own apartment. Good riddance.

Polly had always been as messy as sin. She had always been terrible at cleaning up after herself and she seemed to thrive in chaos, as opposed to cleanliness. I went into the kitchen earlier in the afternoon to pour a long-freezing cup of tea that she had made for me an hour or so before into the sink and found myself nearly heaving. The sink was full to the brim with three days' worth of dishes; most of the plates hadn't even been scraped clean, so they were practically congealing for the most part before me. My hair was starting to escape its bun, I hurriedly whipped it back again from my face before pulling up my sleeves and beginning the laborious and unpleasant job of tackling dishes that had been left *soaking* for that long. Left abandoned, more like. Well, I knew how the poor dirty plates felt. Once I'd dried them and stored them all away, I went into the living room. I was rather surprised that Polly hadn't appeared yet. I barely had five minutes elapse now before she'd poke her head around the door, gawking at me. She had always alarmingly resembled, Big Bird from "*Sesame Street*", right from when she'd been a child. She had always been a nosy old bird too; that usually couldn't bear to let two minutes pass by, without sticking her nasty beak into my business. I could hear her out in the hallway, talking to someone on the phone. I didn't care in the slightest as to who it was that she was talking to as long as she stayed out of my way, I was more than happy to leave her to it.

I looked at the television, it was laden with dust. I couldn't stand dust. Jamie always sneezed like crazy if there was too much dust, he had some type of allergy. I couldn't bear it, I had to clean the TV. I started to manically polish the TV. I pretended that if I polished the TV well enough, I would hear Jamie coming down the stairs. He'd bound down the stairs, he'd burst into the room and he'd beam his "I'm right here" smile. If I could only get the television spotless enough, I could get it to happen, I really could. The polish had started to make my eyes water and my throat tickle. But I couldn't be deterred. I couldn't give up; not when there was so much at stake. I stood back and looked at the TV; it really did look pristine. Any minute now, any minute now…

The living room door opened and I felt that my heart skipped a beat. It was Jamie; it was Jamie; it was Jamie…

It was Adam. I felt briefly breathless with disappointment.

"I was just at the co-op, Mum," he said.

I looked at him blankly. I had no idea he'd even left the house. I didn't care; he was distracting me. I'd polish the TV again and then I would look through all of Jamie's photographs.

"I ran into Karen and Geoff when I was there," he said.

"They were asking after you. You're constantly on both of their minds. They were so desperate to see you, they were telling me how they were on their way now. They're in the hallway now…"

He'd barely finished his sentence before Karen came hurtling into the room; yanking Geoff along by the hand behind her. Karen's auburn hair was pulled back behind her head and secured in a tortoise-shell clasp. Her make-up was lily white; her lipstick pale peach. It looked like the lipstick I'd given her for her birthday. The gorgeous Charlotte Tilbury one, I'd last seen her wearing that when she'd attended Jamie's 21st. She and Geoff had ended up having a massive argument. He'd wound up leaving in a huff before 10:00 pm and Karen had ended up getting so drunk, that she was ever so slightly sick in her new handbag, that matched her shoes so perfectly. Karen looked at me, she took in my appearance and looked fleetingly horrified. Geoff looked a startling shade of purple; he'd never been brilliant at dealing with his emotions.

Karen shocked me by suddenly starting to bawl. She looked mortified by her abrupt show of upset. I registered her desperately trying to muffle her sobs by shoving her fist to her mouth.

"Oh, Susanna!" she wailed.

She released Geoff from her grasp and came up to me, she wrapped me in a tight embrace. I made no effort to hug her back.

"Suze, I've been your best friend for donkey's years and I really don't have a clue what to say to you, other than that, I am so, so sorry."

I felt briefly dazed. Karen had always been ostentatious but I had forgotten that she could frequently feel like a little "*much*". I found myself feeling somewhat tired even listening to her.

Karen took a step back; she took a huge breath.

"Oh my goodness, beautiful James! You didn't get any better than him, did you?"

Geoff shook his head awkwardly.

"No, you really didn't," he said stiffly.

"Our deepest condolences, Susanna. We're all in such shock. I can't even begin to imagine how you must be feeling at the minute."

Karen shuddered, looking visibly perturbed.

"Don't, don't. If it were Tilly or Greg…"

She winced. Karen had always been prone to a spot of foot-in-mouth disease.

"Suze, that was insensitive, I'm so sorry. I really do feel out of my depth."

Karen chewed her lip; resembling a rabbit.

"I'm terrible when it comes to serious situations, always have been. I'm good at chinwags and chuckles, not anything too heavy."

She looked at me, I knew her well. I was fully aware that she was kicking herself.

"Christ, I've put my foot in it again. I really am an idiot, a prize idiot."

She began to weep a fresh batch of tears.

"I really just can't get my head around it! Jamie being killed in a senseless stabbing incident! Of all of the people, why on earth did it have to be him? He was so good, so kind! It's just so unfair!"

Geoff sighed.

"It's just knocked the wind out of our sails, it really has done. Dear God, I can't even begin to understand how you and young Adam must be feeling. It's just so much to get used to."

I stared at both Karen and Geoff. I knew they were trying really hard to work out what I was thinking but my face bore no expression; much to their frustration, I was unreadable.

"You get used to things like the kitchen tap always dripping, your favourite Netflix series coming to an end."

I could feel myself, much to my own irritation, starting to involuntarily shake.

"I will never, ever, get *used* to the fact that my son has been killed! That he's…"

I clutched the back of the sofa; trying to regain my breath.

"DEAD," I uttered, the word escaping me in a choked struggle.

Karen put her hand to her mouth.

"It's so heart-breaking Susanna, I know."

She attempted to hug me again, but I turned around. I made it plain that I did not reciprocate the gesture; that I wanted her to back off. There was a temporary, excruciating silence. I expected Karen to fill it, but to my surprise, it was Geoff that took it upon himself to pipe up.

"Tilly and Greg… they were floored when they found out about Jamie. Gobsmacked, they were. And both of them are absolutely gutted that they couldn't call around with us today. But Tilly…you know how tough she found it at Nottingham, to begin with. She's only just got settled into Uni really, the best part of a year in. I thought it might knock her off her stride, her only coming back for a few days."

I couldn't believe what I had heard. It turned out that that was just the icing on top of the cake. Karen decided to provide the cherry.

"Yes, we thought it was for the best, what with the poor petal having always been prone to a bit of wobbliness. As for Greg, he's still really overwhelmed, to be honest, Susanna. He's finding it hard to take it all in. We decided that with that in mind, it was best he stayed at home."

I turned slowly around to face them, my face like thunder.

"That's sweet. I'm glad that jittery little Matilda is out of the way in Nottingham, away from the supposedly contagious grieving Mother and all the general misery," I sniped.

"Perish the thought of the inconvenience of my son being murdered, meaning that she has another little nervous episode!"

Karen and Geoff looked wounded for an instant. Little did they know that I was just clearing my throat.

"Selective memory, it's a funny concept really, isn't it?" I said, my tone bitter and hostile.

"My goodness, when I THINK of all the times that Jamie waded in for Tilly at school. When I think of all of the little *bitches* that he told to back off, so that wet little Tilly could be left alone. She was viewed as the bloody *loser*, yet he couldn't have given a flying flute about what anyone else thought about her. He always took the time to stop with her; to make the effort."

I glared at them.

"So, I'm glad that little Tills is clearly loving Uni life so much after her *two* faffy gap years where she spent most of that time trailing after Jamie like some sad sap, that she's decided to leave him out to dry, the way he so *easily* could have done with her years ago. I wish to Christ, he had done."

Karen looked tearful.

"Tilly *adored* Jamie, Susanna. She's all through herself, you know that she always held a little candle for Jamie. Well, he was just so loveable, wasn't he?" she said desperately, as she looked around at Geoff; at Adam; at Polly who had now walked into the room, looking tense.

I felt furious.

"Jamie's barely *dead* and you've already got very used to talking about him in the past tense, haven't you? I can imagine all of the vultures poring over what's happened, you know. Insinuating to their own kids that my J lived the gangster lifestyle; that he somehow 'had this coming to him'."

I could feel the tears brimming in my eyes.

"My Jamie spent his whole life protecting people. He looked after others because he was loving and good-hearted. He went out one night to a bar, like any other guy his age. Except all of those other guys his age went home, they had that luxury. Jamie didn't. He wound up getting stabbed because he defended his bloody girlfriend from being groped. The THUG that killed my boy…"

I found myself properly sobbing. Karen was silently weeping; she looked in great pain.

"That monster deserves to ROT," I snarled.

Geoff stared at his feet.

"Whoever is responsible, well, they will be brought to justice, Susanna."

I stared at him, in open-mouthed disbelief. Surely, he couldn't actually be serious? Surely not?

"Justice? There will never, ever be justice because even if they catch that animal and lock him up and throw away the key, Jamie will still be dead!"

Adam started to cry; he was trying to generate as much sympathy as possible from Karen and Geoff. Karen looked startled; it was as though she had only just noticed him.

"Oh Adam, you poor lovie. None of this must seem real. You're too young to have to face all of this; it's such an awful lot for someone your age to have to take in. You just keep standing strong for your Mum, flower. She's going to need you more than ever now."

I felt seething, my teeth were practically chattering with rage. Polly saw my fury, she looked ill at ease.

"Susanna, why don't you come to the kitchen with me and you can help me prepare some lunch for everyone? We'll make my legendary BLTs."

Karen patted her stomach as though she was Mrs Claus.

"Oh Polly, that's so sweet of you. But I really have lost my appetite since I heard the news about Jamie. I just have such a lump in my throat all the time, it's terrible."

This was so patronising; I physically felt my body react. Polly looked over in my direction apprehensively.

"Speaking of food, we brought over some meals," Geoff mumbled.

Karen took my hand. It felt limp.

"I thought that cooking would be the last thing on your mind at the moment, Susanna. Take-outs are all well and good for a few nights or so, but I thought that you could do with some proper home cooking. I made some of your favourites – chicken pie, spag bol. I even had a stab at making some Beef Wellington."

She looked the picture of embarrassment at her word choice. I resisted the urge to scream. It was getting all the more agitating by the second.

Polly rubbed Karen's shoulder.

"Thanks, that was so thoughtful of you both. You're a true friend, Karen."

Karen smiled back at her, grateful for the engagement. She had always been quite needy in that regard. I'd never really minded until today. I felt I couldn't even look at her; I had to turn away; I needed to take a breath.

"Right, Karen, I think we'd best be making a move," Geoff said, sounding pained.

"Don't you think we've been getting under Susanna's feet for long enough now?"

"Yes, yes, we'll get out of your hair now, Susanna," a flustered Karen gabbled.

She hugged me quickly; she smelt of her oh-so-familiar Chanel No5 and there was a very faint aroma of chicken pie.

"I am always here, my love. Day or night, if you want to talk things through, you can give me a bell whenever."

I stared at her mutely. Geoff looked as though he was about to combust.

"Right, don't let me hold you back. You must be chomping at the bit to get home now; back to your family," I said snippily.

Karen looked slightly embarrassed; she tilted her head to one side as though I was a normally well-behaved puppy that had just decided to bare my teeth, out of the blue.

"Can I stop by again tomorrow, Suze?" she asked.

She lowered her tone.

"Just me this time, no Geoff in toe. A nice girly catch up, does that sound like a good idea?"

I felt my eyes roll like marbles. She made it sound like a take-away pizza, a few rom-coms and a good moan were going to make everything all okay. She really didn't have the faintest idea as to what I was going through; all I was ever really going to feel.

“Why don’t you just go home and focus on your kids?” I posed pointily.

Karen knew she was fighting a losing battle. She left the room after casting a wan smile in my vague direction and she sidled out of the room, defeated. Geoff had already dived out of the living room door. Wild horses wouldn’t have stopped him from escaping. Maddeningly, I heard Polly apologising to them on my behalf out in the hallway; chuntering on about me in hushed tones. How dare they!

I turned my back on the living room door and returned to polishing the TV. A solitary tear rolled down my face.

Now

I sat in the living room, scanning through photographs of Jamie meticulously. I found a photo taken on the morning of his first day of secondary school. He and Max are standing outside the house; in blazers that practically trailed down to their knees with rucksacks that made them resemble two little tortoises, off on a big adventure. I had fretted so much about Jamie's first day of secondary school. I had been reassured that he'd have Max by his side as the pair of them had always been as thick as thieves, but I think that any mother that claims she didn't give her child's transition from primary school to secondary school a second thought, is a liar. I need not have fretted though. Jamie had breezed through his first day and came racing back after school with Max; excitedly chattering to me about all of the new friends he'd met, how he and Max were in the same form class, how they'd both had a whale of a time. He'd munched enthusiastically on the brownies that I'd baked them both and told me that he knew I'd have been worrying non-stop about him all day, but I really didn't have to. He was happy; he was safe, and he was having the time of his life. I needed to learn to stop stressing all of the time. I felt tears brimming over; they slid down my face; they very nearly splashed on to the photograph. It felt like yesterday, that Jamie was sitting at the kitchen table with Max, demolishing home-baked treats and enthusing about his first day of Year Seven. I so badly wished that it really was yesterday, as then he'd still be little and I never let him go any further than the corner shop on his own then. He and Max were allowed to go to the corner shop together to buy chocolate and they were allowed to play with the kids on the same road either in our garden or one of theirs, but that was it. It was so much easier then. I didn't have to think of bars and murderers then. I seemed to think of little else now, as much as I tried my level best to do otherwise.

I looked at a photograph of Jamie, dressed up as Danny Zuko, Rachel beside him as Sandie. Jamie looked so happy, glowing, carefree, and gratified. I stared at this photograph hard; it hadn't even been taken that long before Jamie had died. Perhaps about six weeks beforehand; around that time. They say that photographs are worth 1000 words. *Happy,* is certainly the word that sprung to my mind when I looked at Jamie. That was the memory of him that I wanted to have etched into my mind. Not the other memory. Not the one of him…

I shuddered, I couldn't bear to think about it, I really couldn't. I reached over for the bottle of wine. I took a swift swig and then I tried to settle myself once more so that I could really concentrate on all of the photographs. I spread them all out around me so that I could see them all properly. There was no point in having them all in piles. I liked the thought of being able to shroud myself in Jamie's memory.

I felt exhausted but strangely wired as I made a point of looking closely at every single photograph there. Polly came into the room, armed as usual, with a cup of tea. That's Polly all over. Someone's been born, cue tea. Someone's got married, cue tea. Your child's been stabbed to death, cue tea. I privately mused if Polly ever experienced palpitations because she drank so much tea. She'd never *said*, but then there was a great deal that we didn't say to each other. I felt she must be made up of about 90% tea at this stage.

She nearly went flying; she seemed to lose her footing as she came into the room. I think that she tripped over some photos as she came into the room. She really is a klutz; she should take care as to not be so clumsy. She could have stepped on some of Jamie's photos, she could have poured her blessed tea all over them. If she had done either, she'd have found herself on my doorstep with a flea in her ear and doused in her sacred tea. Polly swore under her breath and steadied herself. I ignored her. She made a great performance out of putting the cup of tea onto the mantelpiece and then sitting down on the sofa nearby. I didn't pay her any attention, but it was quite clear that she wanted to broach something with me.

"Hey, Susanna, I was having a think about all of these photographs," she said tentatively.

She gestured at the masses of grinning Jamie's.

"How about we make a great big collage? Then we can clear some space on the floor… have the place a bit tidier…"

I looked at her; silently simmering.

"Sorry, Polly," I said sarcastically. Polly's shoulders slumped.

"Are the photos of Jamie in MY house making the place look less…"

I waved my hand around, trying to find the right word.

“PRESENTABLE?” I hissed.

Polly rubbed her face wearily.

“No, I only meant that it might actually be cathartic. Choosing your favourite photographs of Jamie, to go in a collage that we could hang up in here, maybe. Pride of place, of course.”

She was pretending to be as sweet as pie, but her rancid thoughtlessness was flooring. Sometimes I was shocked, that even after having known her for so long, I was even surprised at this point.

I shook my head.

“How on EARTH would that be cathartic? Photos are all I have left of my son, memories. I want to spend every waking moment, looking *back,* as that was when life was GOOD; when it was actually worth living. Jamie was still alive and back then, I didn’t feel like my heart had just been ripped out.”

Polly looked at me sadly.

“Do you want me to look through them with you? It might be nice to reminisce together.”

I glared at her. Polly was sterling now at pretending that she had been a really hands-on Aunt that would have walked over hot coals for Jamie. She seemed to have a selective memory. She appeared to have forgotten how when both Jamie and Adam were small; I had pleaded with her to be their guardian in the unfortunate event of my death. This had been playing on my mind massively, as at the time, a colleague of mine, had recently died of breast cancer. Maria had been a caring and loving woman, and her death was made all the more tragic, due to the three young daughters who were utterly devastated by her loss. Maria had been separated from her husband, when she tragically died, but he had always maintained an excellent relationship with all of the girls. They went to live with him and his new partner after their Mother’s death. As gut wrenching as the circumstances were, everybody that had known Maria breathed out an enormous sigh of relief that her three beloved daughters were in such safe hands; their father could not have been more capable and devoted. It prompted me to enter a state of panic about who would step up to care for the boys, in the event that anything ever happened to me. I knew that my parents adored their grandsons, but I was extremely conscious of my father’s ailing health and his increased sense of frailty, and worried if it would be too great an ask of my parents, to expect them both to care for the boys, full-time. In many respects, Polly had seemed like the obvious candidate to ask. However, I had not been met with the reception that I had been hoping for. For instance, she had demanded to know if she'd be expected to fork out for the two of them out of her own pocket, as after all, she was a single woman with no children herself and she was used to only having to think of number one. This appeared to be her main concern. I had continually explained to her that I felt it would be better for a younger relative to look after the boys if I was to die and would rather that she ideally did it, with my parents' support, as opposed to the other way around. Polly didn't want to listen to this. She just wanted to know what way it would work money-wise. She'd changed her tune slightly when she discovered that I had a pretty good life insurance. I begged her to step up; I knew at that point that Dean wasn't going to hang around. I knew he wouldn't desert Jamie but I was fully aware of how much he struggled with Adam. I wanted peace of mind; reassurance. Polly deliberated aloud over the phone to me, she actually mused over what she'd spend the lump sum on. Probably a really good car, maybe even a Range. A white one of course; that was the car she'd always wanted. I couldn't believe she could be so heartless to toy with me over something so pressing; so serious. I reinforced that the boys would be no trouble, but she wasn't convinced. She said, "All right then," after a good hour or so of my pleading and grovelling, in a tone that suggested she'd use the money to go on a plush holiday to St Lucia, get a good car, a Mulberry handbag perhaps, before dumping the kids indefinitely at my parents', for them to look after them.

I contemplated reminiscing about this touching little memory, but I couldn't be bothered to even have to interact with her for long.

I simply opted to glare at her contemptuously.

"Why on earth would I want to reminisce with you?" I snapped.

The doorbell rang; sudden and screeching. I ignored it. Polly, however, leapt to her feet and rushed to answer it. She seemed thankful to have an excuse to leave me. She sounded flustered as she spoke to someone in the hallway.

"Oh, my goodness, hello," she said. It sounded as though she had genuinely been caught unawares.

Mumbling took place in the hallway. I didn't care. I wasn't the least bit interested in who she was colluding with, Polly had always been a colluder. I had unfortunately become accustomed to her conspiring ways. I carried on looking at photographs of Jamie, I wanted to feel closer to him somehow.

Polly opened the living room door and hovered a second, before speaking.

"Susanna?" she said gently, as she peered at me dolefully.

I blanked her, I hoped that she'd take the hint and push off, but she persevered.

"Susanna?" she repeated loudly, as though I was deaf.

I looked down at a photograph of Jamie on his first birthday; sitting in front of his Colin the Caterpillar cake, with a huge grin on his face. He'd just had a haircut the day before and he looked cuter than ever.

Polly sighed tiredly.

"Susanna, can you look at me, please?"

I turned around half-heartedly in her direction; reluctant and reproachful.

Polly stepped aside and Rachel tentatively edged her way into the room.

"Hi Susanna," she said nervously.

I looked at her coldly. Rachel shifted under my gaze; she flushed a startling shade of red. She really did look awful. She was normally such a knockout; a real head-turner but today she looked dismal. Her skin looked as though it had been scrubbed red-raw; her eyes were puffy and blood-shot and her long hair hung at the nape of her neck in a limp ponytail. Polly patted her shoulder. She clearly sensed her discomfort. It must have been truly palpable for her to pick up on it because she wasn't exactly the brightest colour in the rainbow.

"It was a bad idea to come," Rachel said shakily.

"I'm sorry," she stammered, as she made for the door.

"I'm really sorry, I should go."

Polly wrapped an arm around her; she assured her that she was very welcome; it was really nice that she had come around. Polly looked fleetingly emotional.

"I think that Jamie would be so happy to know that his two favourite women are still spending time together. Even if he's not here…"

At this, Rachel starts blubbering. Polly went to rub her arm. Rachel misinterpreted the gesture and clung on to her like a little monkey.

"I'm sorry, I'm sorry! I feel like such a mess, I can't even hear his name without crying my eyes out. God knows when I'll actually be able to hear stories about him without turning into a wreck."

She sat down on the sofa, still howling. The sound was siren-like. Polly smiled knowingly.

"It's not going to happen overnight, treasure. But it will, one day. I think Jamie would want us to have a good giggle at his escapades if it meant that we all stopped feeling so dreadful for five minutes."

This struck me as such an absurd comment to utter, even by her standards.

"I'm sure that Jamie would rather still be alive," I said simply.

A mammoth silence descended upon the room. Rachel looked terrified; her eyes as wide as dinner plates as she hugged her knees to her body. Polly sighed heavily, as if unsure of what to say. It was actually Rachel that broke the silence.

"Sometimes I think he's still alive, you know," she imparted suddenly.

"My mobile will ring and I'll convince myself that it's him calling. Even though I know…"

Her voice cracked slightly.

"That it can't be. And sometimes I'll just sit for hours and scroll through all of his social media accounts. I know that he'll never post anything else, so it's like that's the last little window into his head. I feel like I have to memorise every single post, as they're all words that he wrote."

She laughed, although the sound was empty.

"Does that make me sound really stupid?" she questioned, as she looked at myself and Polly, wide-eyed and woe begone.

Polly shook her head. She assured her that that was perfectly normal; it was all part of the grieving process. Polly really did think that she was *it*, whatever it was! She really was so delusional and self-obsessed to believe that she was actually a figure that was in a position to actually give advice. She seemed to perceive herself as being a credible enough human being where people could actually be bothered to listen to her pearls of wisdom. I resented having to be in the same space with both her and Rachel.

Polly suddenly slapped her legs with her hands.

"Right, a cup of tea. Cup of tea," she burbled to herself as she shimmied off to the kitchen. Polly-put-the-kettle-on. The story of her life.

Rachel looked longingly after Polly. She was blatantly frightened at the prospect of having to sit in a room alone with me. I tried to merely ignore her so I could carry on looking at all of the photographs but Rachel emitted flighty and irregular energy; that subsequently had quite a distracting effect. I couldn't concentrate. It really infuriated me that she had just rolled up here uninvited. Surely, she could go and sit with her own friends and family? It was totally out of order; her bestowing herself upon me like this, with not so much as five minutes' notice provided. I felt no desire whatsoever to make conversation with her, but Rachel clearly found the silence unendurable.

"Jamie saved me, you know," she said, her words tumbling out of her like wool that was coming undone.

"Not just in the *obvious* way. He saved me from me if that makes sense. I could be superficial and shallow before I met him. The classic only child I suppose, fussed over far too much."

She flicked her ponytail over one shoulder. Despite her hair looking lifeless and resembling a strange dishwater colour, I saw a flash of the minxy schoolgirl she had been, carelessly catty. I felt my walls go up even more, despite having simply not thought that possible earlier. Rachel pulled at a hangnail briefly on her thumb, before continuing.

"I dated Jamie and I suppose he taught me that STUFF didn't make me happy, going to OTT places with OTT people and plastering it all over Instagram didn't make me happy. "

She laughed, although the sound escapes her in a sob.

"He taught me that being kind and selfless was all that would fill the hole, I'd seemed to have for God knows how long. He showed me what happiness really was."

Rachel bit her lip.

"But now Jamie's not here, I feel like I won't be happy again. I feel so miserable all the time. I guess it's been a shock how many so-called friends have taken such a back seat in terms of actually being there for me. Even my parents have been pretty impatient with me. They see it that I've had a cry and a vent and that I should start moving on; looking forward."

She sobbed, tears trickling down her face, splashing her olive-green jumper.

"But I don't want to look forward. Even the thought of one more *day* without Jamie is unthinkable."

She dabbed at her eyes with a tissue.

"I just adored him. I still do. The thought of ever moving on…"

She shuddered.

"No-no. I just couldn't. Ever. No way."

I didn't respond. Rachel seemed to have worn herself out. She didn't say anything for a second, but she looked visibly relieved to see Polly return, with a tray laden with tea and biscuits. Rachel received her cup of tea gratefully. I stared at mine, as though Polly had poured me a cup of cold sick. She looked at me disapprovingly. She wanted me to get up off the floor and sit on the sofa, sipping tea with her and Rachel. They may be content with sitting there like two old maids but I sure as hell wasn't. Rachel and Polly talked amongst themselves, laughing at how Jamie used to be able to drink a gallon of tea in one sitting; he loved the stuff.

"I just miss him so, so much," Rachel said feebly.

Polly made an effort to comfort her. I watched them both; deadpan.

Rachel pulled away from the hug and looked directly at me.

"Sorry, sorry, Susanna. You must think I'm so pathetic."

I looked at her for a minute or so, non-committal.

"I don't think you're pathetic," I said calmly.

Polly looked pleased, she seemed to be happy that I had actually engaged with Rachel. The tension in Rachel's hunched shoulders seemed to subside slightly.

"To be honest though, Rachel, I don't really care what you feel."

Rachel looked stunned. Polly looked aghast.

"Susanna, why on earth would you say such a thing? That's awful," she uttered in an appalling hiss.

I looked at Rachel, dead in the eye.

"That's no reflection on you, by the way, Rachel. I think that you're a perfectly sound girl but the truth is, I don't care how you feel because I know it will only be for the briefest of times."

Rachel looked shell-shocked.

"You're going to feel really sad for a while," I told her.

"You're going to feel very angry at the injustice. But then you, just like everybody, are going to forget. You're going to go from thinking about him all the time, to every few days. Then you'll maybe go a few weeks without thinking about him. That could well gradually turn into months, potentially years."

Rachel jutted her chin out; she sat with her shoulders back.

"I will never forget Jamie," she said assertively.

I shook my head, with an almost serene sense of matter-of-factness.

"You, just like everybody else, Rachel, will inevitably grow weary of the wallowing. Just like them, you WILL move on and you'll live your life. Then when you all feel overcome with the need to be politically correct, you'll say how you're all 'doing it for J'. Because he was the most full-of-life person that you could ever wish to meet. "

I fought the lump in my throat because I needed to deliver this to Rachel, by hook or by crook.

"That is the difference between you and I, Rachel. You, like everybody else, will get the drive to live again. You'll want to seize the day and make new memories, as opposed to sitting around like a lost soul all day. Whereas I…"

My voice cracked, I resented it cracking in front of Rachel.

"I'll never live again. I will exist. Because I don't see a life worth living anymore if Jamie isn't in it."

Rachel stood up.

"Susanna, I do understand exactly what you're going through, you know. We are both mourning, we are both grieving."

This insinuation was just *insulting*! Had she even been listening to a single word that I had just said?

"Do not BEGIN to talk to me about grief, Rachel!" I stormed.

"Yes, it is horrible losing someone you've been in a relationship with. But don't begin to talk to me about grief when I've lost my son. The individual I should have been able to protect, who was a part of me!"

I got to my feet and began to stalk out of the living room, towards the kitchen. I turned to look at Rachel over my shoulder, before leaving.

"I wish you all the best, Rachel, but don't come around here again. Don't."

Rachel wept on the sofa whilst a strained Polly tried to console her. I strode into the kitchen and stared out of the window. I felt hollow.

Then

I stood in the kitchen, staring out of the window at the garden. I'd never been particularly green-fingered and had frequently pondered over whether it might just be easier paving over all of the grass. It would be less maintenance; it would save the grass from aggravating my hay fever come the summer months. I was glad that I hadn't paved it over. Jamie had loved the garden, right from when he was no age. He loved playing in it, whatever the weather, when he was a young boy. He used to sprint around with Max; playing elaborate games that had been known to span days. When Dean decided to buy Jamie a puppy for his sixth birthday (without consulting me, may I add!), he used to love running around outside for hours on end with Mr Jones. He was a lovely dog and we all loved him dearly. He was a gorgeous golden Labrador with almond-brown eyes that were wide and trusting. I remembered the anger I'd felt when Dean told me simply on the day of Jamie's birthday that he'd been out in the small hours to collect Jamie's puppy, that he knew he would just be over the moon with. I remember being so cross that Dean would make such a big decision, without even waiting to ask if I gave it the go-ahead. After all, I knew that I'd be the one who'd end up being the poor sap, tasked with all of the jobs that go with the territory of having a dog. However, my mind changed in an instant when I saw Mr Jones. He was loving and affectionate and Dean was right. I knew that Jamie would be tickled pink to finally have a dog, especially as he'd been clamouring for a puppy for years. Jamie and Mr Jones had been firm friends; he had his own dog basket in the kitchen but Mr Jones always ended up sleeping at the foot of Jamie's bed for years. I never once personally *saw* him plodding upstairs to Jamie's room, but he was always there, snoring softly by his best friend's side, whenever I used to go into Jamie's bedroom in the morning, to wake him for school.

Mr Jones spent most of his time sleeping now. He was a very old dog and he grew tired very easily. He wasn't up to going on walks anymore but he pottered around the garden, on occasion if he felt like it. I'd not spent an awful lot of time with Mr Jones since Jamie's death. Despite never being awake for too long at any time, Mr Jones often peered forlornly at me from over the edge of his basket. I often saw tears brimming in his eyes. He missed Jamie and he couldn't understand why he wasn't there. I felt a pang of guilt for not making more effort to spend time with Mr Jones. I knew that Polly made a huge fuss of him and she was forever giving him treats. She'd put aside little morsels of chicken and ham for him to feast on. She always said she just couldn't resist his eyes. She fell hook line and sinker for that gaze of his, every single time. I knew that she offered Mr Jones a walk every single morning, showing him his lead to see if he wanted to go out. He never did. Mr Jones frequently looked in the tholes of depression now. If he wasn't asleep, he looked morose now. I cared deeply for Mr Jones, but I never thought I'd have to see a day, where he outlived Jamie.

I looked across at Mr Jones, lying in his basket, half-asleep. I went over and kneeled down beside him. I remembered only days before his death, Jamie had mused over whether it might be a good idea for us to get a Labrador puppy when Mr Jones was still alive. He thought they might be good company for one another and that Mr Jones would pose as a grandfatherly figure to a young pup. Jamie loved dogs and he'd often expressed when he had sat curled up on the sofa with Mr Jones watching the TV, that he couldn't bear the thought of there ever being a time where there wasn't a dog around the house. Mr Jones had led a far slower-paced life for the last two or three years or so, but he had always felt like such a *necessary* component of our home. We decided that it would be unfair to suddenly bestow a hyperactive pup on poor Mr Jones in his twilight years when all he really wanted was some peace and quiet. However, we'd always vowed, *not to let the grass grow*, so to speak. We'd always agreed that after Mr Jones died, we'd leave it a week or two and get another puppy as we didn't want the house to be a dog-free zone indefinitely. However, I was learning that brilliance could often be irreplaceable.

I gently stroked Mr Jones and he looked up at me; his eyes empathetic and intelligent. It was quite therapeutic. I stroked Mr Jones and allowed my brain to numb; to think of nothing, just for a moment. I felt exhausted all of a sudden. Mr Jones clearly felt the same way as he huddled down in his bed, ready for another snooze. The temporary harmony was soon disrupted.

I noticed that Adam was hovering in the kitchen doorway, pale and putrid.

"Mum?" he said into the silence.

I ignored him. I couldn't stand him speaking to me. Why couldn't he just come into the kitchen, feed his face and *go* without uttering a word to me? He'd done this his whole life. I struggled to see why now should be any different. I tried to freeze him out entirely. I stayed down on the floor with Mr Jones and tried to focus on all of the happy memories that he and Jamie had had together. I remembered Jamie's elated face when Mr Jones as a beautiful puppy was presented to him. I remembered Jamie excitedly teaching him new tricks in the garden; stretched out on the grass in the summer with Mr Jones faithfully by his side, petting him affectionately as he chattered to him warmly.

"You must be shattered, Mum. I heard you pacing about at all hours last night, you're dead on your feet. You should go to bed, even if it's just to get a decent hour or so of sleep," Adam said, suddenly appearing at my shoulder. I couldn't *stick* the close proximity. He placed his hand on my shoulder and I found myself flinching with repulse. Adam soon let me go like I was a hot potato as Polly rushed into the room, looking ruffled.

"Rachel's here, Susanna," she announced.

I couldn't be bothered to look at her. I tried to focus on dear Mr Jones instead.

"Tell her to leave," I said sullenly.

Polly let out a big, exasperated sigh.

"Susanna, I can't do that. I've politely sent her packing the last three days she's been around. It will look awful if we keep batting her off all the time."

That was the difference between Polly and I – she was so bothered about how my every move was perceived publicly, whereas I truly could not give a fig. Rachel had a brass neck showing her face in this house; she had more front than Blackpool to come around here, weeping and wailing all the time. It's interesting that she always glosses over her part to play in that *night.* I looked over at Polly.

"Jamie would still be alive if it wasn't for that blubbering BITCH."

Adam tutted, the personification of spitefulness.

"Come on, Mum, that's below the belt. You can hardly blame Rachel for what happened to Jamie."

I felt myself becoming consumed with contempt and embitterment.

"All I know is that Jamie would still be alive if that selfish, spoilt little prima donna hadn't decided to have another birthday do on Tuesday night."

I rubbed at my head furiously.

“She didn’t *have* to have that do on Tuesday night, did she? She’d already had her birthday celebration, the Saturday beforehand. There was no reason for them to be out on Tuesday night!”

Polly attempted to shush me; conscious that ickle-wickle Rachel might hear and throw a wobbly. Her efforts to silence me only served in making me all the more determined to say my piece. As loudly as I blooming wanted!

“I hate the way that she had Jamie eating out of the palm of her hand! Jamie never said, but I think she always liked to insinuate to him that he’d done well by getting her. She had the solicitor parents, the huge big house on Castle Street, her silly little handbag business. I think she liked to lord it over him sometimes; act as if she was a cut above him somehow!”

I rubbed my eyes fiercely, hating the fact that I was crying.

“I can just picture what she’d have been saying up at that bar too, on *that* night. She’d have been fanning the flames at every opportunity, whispering to Jamie in that stupid, silly voice of hers, that she felt scared, that the lout was really starting to intimidate her. She’d have screamed when he went to touch her boob, as though she was having her leg hacked off and would have manipulated Jamie into intervening! Rachel was the one that made Jamie feel he needed to intervene. She and she alone, accounts for how he even came into contact with that…”

I paused before uttering the following words with anger so potent, it was almost frightening,

“KILLER SCUM.”

Polly bit her lip.

“Susanna, I know how difficult you’re finding all of this. You have a lot of anger, that’s so understandable but you can’t turn it all around on Rachel. There is one killer, aka one person at fault. Jamie *wanted* to go to Rachel’s birthday drinks, he thought the world of her. Nobody could have predicted that that violent menace was going to be there, hell-bent on causing harm.”

Polly tried to take my hand.

“Rachel’s hurting, Susanna, just like you are. Perhaps you should help each other out by being there for one another, instead of pushing her out into the cold all the time.”

I looked at her; lividness contorting my features. Polly looked uneasy.

“Polly, get out of my face right this second and take your so-called *fucking* advice with you!” I blazed at her.

I grinned maliciously.

"Why don't *you* go out and sit with Rachel, eh? That would be a match made in Heaven, two self-obsessed, melodramatic drama-queens together. You can go off and patronise and pontificate until your heart's content with Rachel."

Polly had tears in her eyes. She stared at me pleadingly.

"Susanna, *please* just try and speak to her," she said pleadingly.

"By all means, say you're not up to company at the minute, but say something at least. It has to come from you really, otherwise, she might think that you wouldn't be opposed to talking to her, but it's me that constantly trying to get her to clear off."

Her inability to actually do anything useful was really starting to antagonise me.

"How *dare* you stand there, doling out orders to me! Go off and do something good for once and tell Rachel to…"

Rachel suddenly appeared in the kitchen doorway; blotchy and tear-stained. Her hair was scraped back severely; she didn't have any make-up on, which made her look oddly unfinished. Her lip wobbled.

"Oh Susanna, you don't know how much comfort I get out of being here in this house. I feel like it's impossible to grieve in my house almost. I'm watched all the time and it's always implied that I'm a hopeless case, for just sitting around the house, all day."

Adam reached out and awkwardly patted Rachel's shoulder. She didn't seem to notice; she made no effort to so much as a glance in his direction.

"Being here, being in Jamie's home makes me feel closer to him. Being amongst his belongings; his family. Mr Jones, it just makes me feel as though he's not so far away."

Adam nodded; he was trying to look stoic and subdued. Polly smiled at Rachel sadly. I couldn't believe it. Was anyone going to turn around and tell this gaslighting bimbo how it was? It appeared not. I cleared my throat. They do say that if you want a job done, you should do it yourself after all.

I stepped forward, my face revealing my incredulousness and vexedness.

"R*eally*? Really, Rachel? Do you actually expect me to stand here and swallow all that up?"

Rachel looked as though the rug had been yanked from beneath her feet.

"Sorry, what?" she said, shocked and stammering.

I shook my head; my intolerance of her was plain to see.

"It's all very sweet how you like traipsing around here all the time. Doing your little-girl-lost act whilst you expect hot cocoa and hugs as we pretend to give a shit whilst you moan and drone all day."

Adam feigned indignance.

"Don't be cruel, Mum."

It was getting more farcical by the second. Adam, one of the most twisted and sinister individuals I had ever encountered, had the gall to try and give me the third degree about *cruelty*!

"Don't you dare pipe up again," I snarled at him.

"You really are a vile little loser."

Polly took Adam's hand; she looked at me disappointingly. Rachel was still staring at me, eyes like saucers as she shook like a leaf. I glared at her.

"It's all well and good you feeling nice and cushioned when you come around here. But I don't."

I looked around at the kitchen.

"Being here reminds me that my gorgeous J isn't coming home. He's never going to walk in that door again, grinning and joking. He's never going to see him mucking around again, having a laugh, living his life."

My eyes narrowed.

"And I blame you for that, Rachel."

Rachel looked horrified, she exclaimed that she simply couldn't fathom how I could think such a thing.

"You were always so GREEDY, so demanding. You couldn't accept that you'd already had a big birthday bash. You wouldn't rest until you'd had celebration number two. What on earth would possess you to decide to have another birthday do on Tuesday night?"

Rachel quivered; hanging her head.

"No wonder you look like crap," I hissed.

"So, you flaming should! Jamie would never have crossed paths with that murderer if it hadn't been for you, Rachel! If you'd not stood there, egging on that killer to come wandering up to make a pass at you, Jamie would never have been stabbed! Jamie paid the ultimate price for your ego boost, you loved getting male attention, you got a kick out of trying to make him jealous! So well fucking done, Rachel. He would never have crossed paths with that murderer if it hadn't been for you!"

I was aware that my hiss had built up to a scream. Rachel backed away from me, as though I was the "Wicked Witch of the West". Polly suggested softly to Rachel that it might be an idea if she went home, things were still very fresh here and I probably needed some time to digest what had happened privately, before having anyone around the house. As Rachel turned to leave out of the door, Adam reached across to touch her. His hand deliberately landed on the exposed skin, where her jeans met her jumper. Rachel flinched briefly, clearly uncomfortable. Adam smiled at her faux innocently, pretending to be the picture of empathy. I felt sickened.

Rachel left; Polly accompanied her to the door. Adam loitered in the kitchen doorway. I looked at him with disgust. How could it even be true that someone as malevolent as him was here instead of someone as remarkable as Jamie? Adam seemed to sense my fury palpably and he slunk away. I returned to sitting on the floor again. Mr Jones' tail wagged slightly as I petted him. It was coming to something when I felt that he was the best source of comfort that I had; the only one who was unfalteringly there for me.

Now

I bustled to the table, cradling two plates loaded with chicken pie, mash and vegetables. Mr Jones circled my feet. He'd always loved the smell of chicken. He was acting like a puppy again, going this way and that, making me step over him. This was his tactic, he'd only get out of my way once he'd been handed a hunk of chicken.

"You are a daft old beggar," I told him teasingly. Still, I could never resist Mr Jones. I managed to place the two plates on the table and cut open my own pie. I pulled out a considerable chunk of chicken.

"Happy now?" I asked Mr Jones, as he gobbled it out of my hand, munching appreciatively. He seemed very pleased with himself, he wandered off back to bed, looking full and contended. *Good food, good mood* that had always been Mr Jones' outlook.

Max smiled.

"Mr Jones looks like the cat that got the cream. Well, the dog that got the chicken."

We both laughed.

It was strange, this was one of the first times since Jamie's death that I actually didn't feel paralysed with grief. Having Max there, was a little bit like having a small piece of Jamie still with me. He really was the cheese to his cracker; the yin to his yang. Physically, they weren't dissimilar. Max was an inch or so shorter than Jamie, he wasn't quite as broad, and his hair was more wavy than curly. Max had always joked that he was the *budget* version of Jamie. He was frequently dubbed as Jamie's understudy, as girls that had made a play for Jamie who'd found themselves being courteously declined, more often than not found themselves making a beeline for Max. He was seen as the *next best thing*, the credible second best. It always amazed me that this genuinely never seemed to bother Max. You would have expected it to be hard, feeling as though you were always playing second fiddle to your best friend all the time. However, it never seemed to be something that had troubled him. Jamie had always been revered by Max but this was a power dynamic that Jamie never would have dreamed of taking advantage of. If Jamie had had a different personality, it could have easily been a case that he was the leader, and Max was merely the led. However, that simply wasn't in Jamie's nature. Jamie always treated Max with the respect and compassion that best friends should. From being no age, Jamie assessed that Max had difficulties at home. His parents didn't deserve him; they never so much as tried to look after him properly. Max used to arrive in Reception class in stained school jumpers and unclean school shirts, always looking dishevelled and somewhat shell-shocked. Even at that age, some of the children started making unkind comments. One particularly nasty boy made a horrid habit out of pinching his nose whenever Max walked by. Jamie, from there on out, took it as his job to defend Max against anyone and he was fiercely loyal to him. Some longstanding primary school friendships start to fade somewhat as children pass through into secondary school, but that was certainly far from true, in Jamie and Max's case. If anything, time seemed to make their bond all the more unbreakable.

That was why it was good to share a meal with Max, to spend some time with him.

"Sorry for bombarding you with texts all the time, Susanna," Max said as he started to ravenously tuck into his pie.

"I just want you to know that I'm always thinking of you. I hated the thought of you thinking me terrible for having not physically called around as much as I would have liked to, but I was just so scared of getting in the way. But it's really nice being here, having dinner with you. It's just like old times."

I laughed.

"Hey, I've only asked you around to try and get rid of some of this food."

I made an effort to try and eat; I had a bite or two of mashed potato, knowing that Max was watching me.

"Honestly, people can't bear to converse with me for five minutes but they bring around the food equivalent of Mount Everest on a regular basis."

Max looked deep in thought. It looked as though he was about to say something but then thought better of it. Instead, he settled for, "Well, whoever made this chicken pie has surpassed themselves."

"I think Karen made this," I said.

I rolled my eyes.

"I'll tell her that her blooming pie got your seal of approval. She always likes her ego being massaged."

Max laughed.

"Her voice may be like nails on a chalkboard, Susanna, but she cares about you. She's trying. I think half the battle is people not having a clue what to say to you."

I took a sip of water.

"The thing is, I don't want swarms of people milling around like how they did in the really early days; as annoying and frustrating as a fly. They usually just turn up once anyway so they can tell people that they've shown their face and then I don't see them for dust again."

I shrugged.

"I guess I'd rather that they just didn't turn up at all if they were just going to disappear at the drop of a hat."

Max nodded; he was clearly in agreement.

"I like having you here," I said sincerely.

"Never feel like you're intruding, you're always welcome to come around whenever you please."

Max looked suddenly emotional.

"Jamie was the brother I never had, Susanna. He was my partner in crime; the cookies to my milk."

He snorted slightly, although it looked as though he was trying really hard not to cry.

"He was the guy I always wished I could be but I was never jealous of him, weirdly enough. I think I was too busy concentrating on the fact that I had such an amazing best friend."

I nodded, touched.

"You've always been like a Mum to me too, Susanna," Max continued. "My own mother was always drugged up to her eyeballs and the less said of my dad, the better."

He looked emotional.

"Don't think I'll ever forget how you virtually took me in. I mean, I kind of unofficially lived here. You never made me feel like a burden though. I always felt so included, so a part of things. I mean, Jamie always felt like my *brother*."

He rubbed his eyes.

"This…this…grief."

He waved his hand about, searching for the right words.

“It’s not the grief you feel for a mate. It’s the grief you feel for a family member.”

I took his hand as he started to cry.

“I know, sweetheart, I know. You’ve always been a part of this family. I always classed you as an extra son. I mean, you and J were always like two peas in a pod.”

The kitchen door opened suddenly.

It was Adam. He walked in; thwarted and jaded. Max had never been a fan of Adam’s. He could pass the time of day with him but he was suspicious of him, he wouldn’t trust him as far as he could throw him.

“All right, Adam?” Max said. It was objectively a polite addressal, but Max uttered the words somewhat gingerly. It was abundant that he didn’t particularly want to have to engage with him.

Adam nodded.

“Yeah, I’m ticking along. Yourself?”

“Just grubbing up with your mum. Appreciating Karen’s culinary skills.”

Adam attempted to smile. I was aware that he was trying to get eye contact with me. It revolted me that he constantly had to try and taint any tiny okay moment I had on any day. Why couldn’t he just push off and leave me to sit and have a meal with Max, without constantly having to try and ruin things?

“Hi, Mum,” Adam slimed.

I decided that simply not entertaining him conversationally whatsoever was probably the best course of action. I blanked him and smiled across the table at Max.

“I think there was a tragic poignancy in the fact that it was you who broke the news to me about J.”

I sighed.

“I know that technically Rachel said first, but I just felt in an utter daze, I couldn’t take it in. I feel it was hearing it from you that made it sink in.”

Adam looked disgruntled.

“I told you too. When you sat in the hallway, crying. I told you too.”

My lip curled; he really was shameless! He still wanted a cameo in the narrative of me finding out that Jamie had been murdered! Were there really no ends to his insidiousness?

I hadn't uttered a single word to Adam, yet the look on my face clearly spoke 1000 words. He burst into tears, all for Max's benefit.

"Oh Adam, there's no need to get upset," Max said awkwardly.

"Your Mum… She…"

He looked as though he was struggling to conjure up something consoling to say.

"Didn't mean anything by it, not really."

Max regarded Adam warily, he seemed to sense that the tears he was shedding could be described as nothing other than *crocodile tears*. I watched Adam briefly with disgust before making an effort to have another bite of my meal, as I looked at Max.

Then

I shuffled around Jamie's bedroom, looking through all of his belongings. I looked at his bookshelf and smiled wanly at the collection of well-thumbed Harry Potter books. Jamie had never been particularly into reading as a child; he used to read a chapter or so of several different books and would put the book down, with every intention of starting it again after he had finished some game he was playing with Max, which never really seemed to materialise. The only books that he'd ever been truly gripped by, had been the Harry Potter collection. He was mesmerised by the world J.K Rowling had created. The books were so engaging, he really felt as though he was at Hogwarts with Harry. He knew a lot of the spells by heart, which he used to enjoy chanting. I remembered he'd written a letter to J.K Rowling when he was a boy, to thank her for writing such exciting books. I couldn't remember if I'd actually sent it, I'd intended to but I always had 1001 things to do and it might have gone clean out of my head. I so hoped I had sent it. Jamie rarely asked for much, but he did ask me to send off that letter. I could have kicked myself – I felt useless. Why on earth didn't I know what had happened to the blasted letter?

I looked at the clothes in his wardrobe. When I moved the clothes, it looked as though there were lots of Jamie's dancing around in his wardrobe. I picked up his cream silk shirt, it still smelt faintly of his aftershave. I couldn't remember the last time he'd worn this. I remembered that this was the shirt that he wore to meet Polly's last boyfriend, about a year ago. Jamie had gone into peals of laughter as the *boyfriend* was four years older than him. He actually remembered him from school. You would have expected Jamie to have fumed at his Aunt – after all, if she was going to act like a lush, she could at least make sure she wasn't cradle-snatching young guys in their early twenties. Jamie found it hilarious – his Aunt, the cougar. He'd always had a fantastic sense of humour. He believed that it was important to always try and see the lighter side of life, where possible. He always joked that "*Life wasn't Burger King. We couldn't always have it our way.*"

Jamie dealt with adversities with skill and wisdom, way beyond his years. He was light-hearted and gregarious, but he was one of the most principled people that I'd ever encountered. When Jamie and Max were in Year Nine, one of the nasty boys twigged that Max's mother was a drug addict. To this day, it's never been discovered whether this boy just spread this around as a malicious rumour; not genuinely knowing that Max's mother was a drug addict or whether he found out somehow that this was the case and posed as the aberrant town crier. Some of the kids in the year turned on Max – they mocked and ridiculed him; they really went to town on this revelation. Jamie always said afterwards that the self-satisfied smirk of the bully was soon wiped off his foul face when he stood up for Max. He made it plain that he didn't want to associate with anyone that thought it was acceptable, to stand there cackling about Max's mum. Jamie said that anyone who thought that Max's circumstances were amusing, could give him a wide berth in future as he made it crystal clear that he didn't want to speak to people that could be so taunting and unsympathetic. Jamie had also told the bully that he was one of the saddest, most pathetic individuals he'd ever met and that he'd pity him if he wasn't so rancid. The bully's mouth gaped open in shock. He'd expected Max to be left high and dry, with everyone turning their backs on him. Max had the last laugh in the end – after Jamie spelt out to the bully exactly what he thought of him, everyone started to keep a distance from the bully. People swerved him on mass, no matter how often he, "apologised", to Max. Jamie said at the time that people like that aren't capable of genuine remorse; their apologies will never be meaningful. Jamie was a born leader and a good leader has integrity; they have heart. I suppose what was so special about Jamie was the fact that he was someone that made everyone feel like a somebody. And you don't meet too many people like that in a lifetime if any.

I found Jamie's school yearbook in his wardrobe. I flicked through the dull pages about staff and school concerts and whatnot until I reached the final section of the yearbook. There were photos of all the different pupils, with messages written underneath by their peers. Max's photo was one of the first photographs that I saw. All of the photographs were in alphabetical order and Max's surname was Abbott, so he was practically first up. At a quick glance, he looked cheeky and careless, but when you looked really closely, you could see the self-consciousness in his smile. I saw Jamie's comment was written beneath:

"Maximillian, I am going to keep this short and sweet as I really don't want this to be as soppy as a sponge. In short, thank you for being my right-hand man. I couldn't imagine going through this crazy thing we call life, without you being by my side. Thanks for being amazing. If you were a celebration chocolate, you'd definitely be the Malteser as opposed to the Bounty. Love you Max, J x."

I found myself welling up. Reading his words did make him seem more alive, more accessible. I flicked through and saw Tilly's page. There weren't a lot of particularly personal comments written there. The vast majority just said things like *Good Luck* and *Bye Tilly*. However, in amongst all of these bland, glib comments which all lacked substance, I saw one that stood out:

"Tills, I want to thank you for being a complete diamond. You're one of the sweetest people I've ever met (and I am pretty sure that the saying 'as sweet as pie' was written about you.) You've always been a dark horse, so I'm pretty sure that you won't confirm this, but I know it's true. I know you are going to go off to some very exciting things but if there's one thing, I've ever said over all the years that you actually take on board, please let it be this – smile, darling. Life really is too short and too sensational not to. Always here for you. Love you girl. J x."

I felt a surge of anger at all of the nurturing compassion that Tilly had always been treated with by Jamie. He'd been stabbed to death and she'd not even come back. It clearly wasn't noteworthy enough to leave university for a week or so over.

I flicked through some of the other pages and found Rachel's. She had the most messages out of all of the girls; they were all gushing and grovelling; clearly, they were all desperate for Queen Bee to keep in touch with them. Jamie had written a comment on Rachel's page. This was before they'd started dating. It was much shorter than a lot of the comments he'd written on everyone else's pages. He'd simply written:

"Good luck with everything Rach J x."

I flicked through until I got to the last page. There he was, Jamie Wright. Last but certainly not least. His page was heaving with comments; it seemed as though the world and its dog had decided to write a message on his page. Rachel had written a huge essay; she'd practically confessed her undying love for him. Tilly had written a twee little message and had doodled a string of hearts, all neatly coloured in with felt-tip pens. I scanned the page, looking for Max's comment. I found it; it was near the bottom.

He had written:

"Jamie, the legend that is! I am putting it in writing that I am low-key begging you not to forget about me when we leave school and you wind up becoming King of the World or something (which obviously you're going to do, no doubt about it!). I'm only joking, I know you won't forget about me! Thanks a million for every single thing that you do because you are the kind of friend that's hard to come by and I never want you to question how much you mean to me. I love you, big man, truly, madly, deeply. Your Maximillian x."

I found myself crying slightly. Reading their camaraderie made Jamie seem all the more alive. It just made it even more difficult to process that someone with a presence so naturally illuminating and enriching, wasn't here anymore.

Polly poked her head around the door.

"Hi," she said softly.

I ignored her.

"Guess who?" said an oh-so-familiar voice as he stepped out from behind her. I instantly felt comforted. It was *Max.*

I ran to him and he wrapped me up in an enormous bear hug. Polly sloped off.

"Susanna, if this is a bad time, please say. The last thing I want to do is to hang around, getting on your nerves. I'd totally get it if you just wanted it to be family," he said thickly.

I looked at him, pretending to be scolding him.

"Will you give over? You are family, sweetheart! You're like a surrogate son to me, I always want you to think of here as your home."

Max looked overcome with emotion as he looked around the room.

"I still can't quite believe he's gone," he whispered.

He gestured around the room.

"Everything's the same, exactly as it was. The only thing that's changed is the fact that J isn't coming back."

He'd barely uttered his sentence, before breaking down in tears. Max had always been stoic, he'd not really been one to majorly show his emotions. You normally had to really worm out what was bothering him, he'd been like that right from having been a young child. Seeing him so devastated before me was heart wrenching.

I hugged him in a natural, maternal manner.

"There, there, sweetheart. I know, I know."

Adam crept into the room. He'd probably been eavesdropping the whole time and had decided to make an appearance. Red-eyed and pasty, he hovered. He was awaiting to be noticed, he was anticipating Max making a huge fuss of him. Polly suddenly reappeared, at his shoulder.

"Hey, Ads," she said cheerily.

"Have you had some breakfast yet?"

Adam shook his head. He was still staring fixated at Max and I. He was desperate to taint the memory and he badly wanted to secure some airtime for himself.

"I'll make you some tea and toast," said Polly to Adam.

"If you keep skipping meals, you'll waste away."

Polly headed off down the stairs, clearly grateful to have something to do.

"God, I'm sorry, Susanna," Max sobbed into my shoulder. "It's ridiculous, me weeping all over you."

He sniffed, looking incredulous.

"Why on earth should you be wiping my eyes when you're the one who's suffering the most? Your kid dying…"

He paused, looking sombre. "That's a form of torture."

I hugged Max tighter.

"Don't feel guilty about being upset, Max. The pair of you were inseparable. You probably feel like you've lost your right arm."

Adam looked sullen.

"I miss Jamie so much," he simpered. He was craving attention – he longed for me to sprint over in placatory mode, the way I'd behaved towards him, right from when he was knee-high to a grasshopper. Well, not anymore.

"His death…I just feel like it's zapped me, you know. I'm just so tired all the time and I just want this horrid feeling in the pit of my stomach to pass. But of course, it won't. Because Jamie's gone for good."

Adam started to bawl. I didn't take him beneath my notice; nor did Max.

"We can help each other as much as we possibly can," I said to Max firmly.

"We both loved Jamie so much."

Polly approached Adam, laden with tea (as usual) and a plate of toast. He took them from her, without uttering a word or even giving her eye contact. His gaze had not left Max and I once.

Now

I sat hunched on the sofa, my legs crossed beneath me like a child. I'd fallen asleep for about half an hour last night and had the most horrific nightmare about Jamie. He wasn't alive in it. If I could dream about him as he *was* as opposed to how he looked at the end, I could at least feel slightly closer to him and all he was. This was the nightmare that was starting to plague me, of Jamie lying there dead. This one wasn't at the mortuary. This one was somehow even worse. It was how he had looked at the undertakers.

I shuddered; I battled the thought away as best as I could. I looked through all of his photographs. I needed to look at them until every single one was etched into my mind. Power in numbers, that's how the saying goes, isn't it? I needed all of Jamie's memories to outnumber and overpower the ghastly nightmares of him at the end. End, I wanted those horrendous nightmares to end. I shook my head, what was I even talking about? Even if those nightmares stopped, I was in a living one that was all encompassing; never-ending.

I had a splitting headache and I felt drained to the degree where I looked physically unwell. I'd recoiled when I caught a glimpse of my reflection in the living room mirror this morning when I'd scuttled down from upstairs. I had gotten good at avoiding looking at myself. I did my level best not to, as the sight I saw before me was always devastating. I didn't even resemble myself anymore, in any way whatsoever. It was like having every tiny aspect of myself stripped. I had been stripped of my whole life, in essence, and had simply been left to flounder in this dystopian abyss. I started to wriggle; I was starting to become so fidgety; so jumpy. My mum had always called Polly a "fidget-bottom" when she was small, she said it used to drive her demented how she never seemed to be able to sit still for two minutes. I was driving myself demented; I tried desperately hard to sit still, but I couldn't seem to, for love nor money. I tried to distract myself. I reached down from the sofa and picked up the bottle of wine lying idly on the floor. I miserably unscrewed it, resigned to my own sorrow and glugged.

Polly came into the room, frowning.

"Really, Susanna? It's half-past eleven in the morning and you're knocking back wine like it's tap water."

I carried on drinking, feeling encumbered with a mixture of rebellion and self-revulsion. Polly folded her arms and scowled at me. If she was trying to look matronly, she was not succeeding. She just resembled one gigantic muppet.

"For goodness' *sake,* Susanna, you're going to make your liver pack up if you keep going at this rate."

She fired me a filthy look.

"Don't think I haven't noticed the amount of booze you've been putting away. I've held my tongue for long enough, but it's getting beyond a joke now, Susanna."

Polly tried to prise the bottle from out of my hands. I couldn't believe her nerve, trying to act all solemn and sensible when for years on end she'd been the reckless wreck that couldn't give a damn about anyone other than herself! I slapped her hands away. Hard.

"Oh, for goodness' sake, Susanna!" she cried, appearing at the end of her tether.

"Will you throw me a bone here?"

Polly's eyes filled with tears. I stared down at the sofa, not wanting to meet her gaze. Why couldn't she just shove off and leave me to it? I'd never pretended to be a shining example of good company. She was usually pretty good indeed at going through life and not giving me a second thought. I failed to see why she'd decided to practically chain herself to my side now. Polly didn't appear as though she was planning on making a sharp exit though, much to my disappointment. She agitatedly ran her hands through her hair.

"I'm exhausted of pussy-footing around you all the time, Susanna! My tongue's practically bleeding, due to biting it so flaming much!"

I took another swig of wine. I stared at the bottle emptily for a second. I despised it passionately, but I needed it; I ached for it all the same. I carried on drinking. Polly made a low, moaning sound like an animal in pain.

"For Christ's sake, Susanna, can you not see what you're doing to yourself?" she posed desperately.

Polly rolled her eyes, her face like thunder.

"I just want to make you see sense, to shake you by the shoulders."

I looked at her levelly. I placed the bottle down on the floor by my feet, my face contorting with fury.

"My world will never be the same again, Polly," I said tightly. My hands balled into fists. "Why bother shaking me by the shoulders as you so nicely put it, when my whole world has been shaken?"

My voice cracked with potent emotion. The sound of this seemed to prompt tears from Polly.

"Susanna, you're turning into a person I hardly recognise. You're confrontational, angry, and BITTER. You've been treating Adam horribly for ages now."

This was almost laughable.

"Poor old Adam, eh?" I interjected frostily.

Polly sighed; she made no secret of her exasperation towards me.

"There you go again, twisting the knife."

She winced, clearly irritated at herself for her choice of wording. I stared at her; aghast and enraged. She pulled back slightly. I think my angst was unsettling her.

"*Me*? Twisting the knife with *Adam*? What the way that SCUM stuck the knife into my Jamie, eh?"

I leapt to my feet. Polly sighed anxiously.

"Do you even remember Jamie, Polly? Because all you seem to do these days is prance around here, flapping about poor FLAMING Adam! You're acting as if he's all hard-done-by in all of this; like he's some sort of *victim.*"

I dissolved into tears.

"Jamie is the victim in all of this and once again that manipulative little USER is trying to get all of the focus shifted onto him! Jamie gets STABBED TO DEATH, yet it's Adam that should be on my mind?"

I rubbed my eyes furiously; they felt like weights in my head. My eyes constantly throbbed now and I detested feeling less awake; feeling like I could sleep all of the time when I *couldn't*, because whenever I closed my eyes, I saw Jamie lying there dead. Usually, I'd drink until I eventually sent myself to sleep, but I'd always wind up having the same nightmare, night after night, without fail.

"My baby was KILLED by some knife-wielding thug that clearly thought he was Clapham's answer to Mr Hard Man. He carried a weapon, thinking he had the right to wave it about and end a life."

My voice had grown shriller and shriller and I could feel my body physically sinking.

"Do you think he'd had his sights set on Jamie the whole night? Do you think that low-life actively set out as to how to get Jamie's attention, so that once he got it, he could turn around and knife him?"

Polly tried to comfort me but I slapped her away.

"My boy was there, unbeknown to him, having the last drinks he'd ever have with his friends. That thug was lurking throughout, he wanted to attack him that night. Jamie was always going to protect Rachel, especially if she was being pawed at, and that's when that lowlife turned and stabbed J."

I tried to regain my composure, as I was sobbing so hard that I could barely talk. Polly tried to dab at my eyes with a tissue but I didn't want her touching me.

"That murderer didn't just take Jamie's life. It is not just Jamie that lies there in that grave of his, it is everybody that loved and cared about him. However, you'll find that with everyone else, there will be a time when they'll all be given some sort of 'Hall Pass' to live. They'll crawl out of the grave and they'll leave Jamie there, on his own."

I shook my head so hard that my neck clicked.

"Not me though," I said adamantly.

"Jamie's life has ended and that, therefore, means that my life has ended too. I'm his MOTHER. If he's dead, then that means that I am as well. Because I feel like I'm just going through the motions now, Polly."

I rubbed my eyes, sniffed fiercely.

"I'm technically still breathing, but I'm dead, let's face it."

I laughed bitterly, tears streaming down my face.

"I'm part of a club that nobody wants to join. I am a fully-fledged member of the Bereaved Parents society. "

Polly looked at me worriedly.

"The Bereaved Parents Society is the club where people whose worlds have crashed in around them pretend that they can live again, whereas really they *can't*. They *can't*, Polly."

"Surely that's all the more reason to keep communicating with Adam," Polly whispered.

"He's still here, Susanna. He should be your motivator, your purpose."

I listened to her, utterly incredulous.

"You're not LISTENING, Polly. You don't seem to grasp the fact that grief doesn't offer you a personality transplant. Adam is still the same toxic, exploitative piece of work that he always has been. I wasted far too much of *Jamie's* precious time fretting and fussing over that depraved little user. Why should I pretend to stand there when he sheds his crocodile tears when there's no point whatsoever?"

I shook my head.

"You act like I've changed into something or someone totally different, Polly, but grief doesn't change you, it *reveals* you. All of my wounds have had the stitches yanked out, all of my scars are open and bleeding."

Polly went to take my hand. I couldn't even describe the wave of vexedness that I felt at her, attempting to paw at me like that!

"I'm sick of being surrounded by INJUSTICE. You being here all the time like Mother Hubbard when you barely set foot over the threshold before – *that's* an injustice in itself! The destructive darkness of Adam overshadowing the light of my J. The fact that Jamie *had* to go to that particular bar for Rachel's birthday drinks when they had the whole of London at their feet! The fact that that murdering *parasite* took a disagreement down a sinister route when he had to involve a knife!"

I crouched to the floor, hugging my knees as I wept.

"Jamie must have been so *scared*. That atrocity of a man will never be given enough jail time if he even *gets given* it."

I looked at Polly, who stared fretfully back at me.

"How on earth can somebody even decide how many years someone's life was worth? That murderer could spend the rest of his life rotting in prison and it would still never be enough."

Polly looked as though she was thinking very hard of something worthwhile to say, you could practically hear the cogs turning in her brain.

"The trial could bring you some sort of closure, Susanna," she said tentatively.

"You'll finally get to see Trav—"

I practically convulsed with outrage.

“Do not dare breathe that name in my house!” I shouted.

Polly took my hand. This time, I didn’t have the energy to pull away.

“We’ll get justice, Susanna, I promise.”

Justice, why did people insist upon throwing that word around as though it was something I could actually achieve? I looked at Polly hopelessly before picking up the bottle of wine again and drinking steadily. She didn’t try to stop me this time.

Then

I sat at the bottom of the staircase, petting Mr Jones. Adam was out in the kitchen. I'd poked my head around the door, but once I had seen that he was there, I'd turned on my heel. I didn't want to have to share the same space as him. Especially not with what he was doing.

He had been chopping chicken when I'd last peered around. I couldn't stand seeing knives; they made me think of Jamie; they made me think of what he'd been murdered with. I loathed the fact that we had numerous knives in the house. Anytime I went out into the kitchen; I felt like I was actively avoiding looking at the murder weapon. Adam didn't seem at all bothered about using them. He had looked as happy as a sandboy, chopping away as though he didn't have a care in the world. He sickened me.

I was sitting at the bottom of the stairs. I really fancied a glass of water but I'd have to wait until he'd gone. Mr Jones had ambled out into the hallway to join me and he was good company. He was non-judgemental; he didn't tut or lecture, whine or gripe. He just let me *be*, he didn't look at me like I was an ogress if I decided to have a drink of wine whenever I pleased. Mr Jones just enjoyed sitting there with me, getting the backs of his ears tickled. I nuzzled my nose on his fur. Unbeknownst to Adam and Polly, who had meandered into the kitchen from the living room, I could hear every word they said.

"I found a big bottle of Pinot under the sofa," I heard Polly announce abruptly to Adam.

"She can think again if she thinks that I'm just going to stand by and let her drink herself silly."

I heard her pour the remaining contents of the bottle down the sink. I felt soured and attacked. I couldn't for the life of me, fathom why she had to keep wading in in her size fives. If I wanted to spend my days drinking on my own, then that was my prerogative. She needed to *back off.*

Then I heard *him* pipe up.

"She will get better, won't she, Polly?" Adam asked.

There was a pause, Polly obviously knew she was way over her head and that she didn't have the slightest clue as to what to say to him.

"Of course, she will," she responded after a very long silence.

"You just wait and see…once the funeral's taken place and the trial's…"

She trailed off. Adam jumped in.

"Polly, I really don't know if she's going to be able to cope being in the same room as him. Let alone being able to sit there whilst that night is relived."

Polly made a silly, humming noise that she always made when she was nervous. She sounded like a barmy bumblebee.

"She's as tough as old boots, your mum. She might well surprise you, Adam. And anyway, she's going to have heaps of support around her. Everybody's going to be rallying around."

I shook my head, listening with disbelief. Mr Jones looked up at me; his stare intent and knowing. I carried on petting him, although my hands shook slightly.

"Once the funeral's taken place and the trials over, everybody can start to move on," Polly said matter-of-factly.

"You watch, it could be then that your mum feels as though she's been given the green light to live again, to try and get back to her old self."

I couldn't stand to hear it anymore.

I marched into the kitchen, Mr Jones padding along stoically behind me. He made his way over to his bed whilst I looked backwards and forwards between Polly and Adam; my dislike penetrating and piercing. Polly seemed unnerved.

"Adam, tell your mum what you're doing over there," she said quickly.

Adam grinned, I found myself resisting the urge to gasp. There was something so unnatural about his smile.

"I'm just in the middle of making us all a chicken casserole for us to have later. I thought it might be nice for us all to sit down and eat together."

My lip curled.

"Only do two portions then – for you and her," I said coldly.

Adam raised his eyebrows.

"Don't be daft, Mum. You'll be starving."

I glared at him.

"I'd sooner eat my own eyeballs than sit around at a table, listening to your poor-me performance. You're very good now at glossing over the fact that you were BORN a vile little gargoyle that loved nothing more than making the atmosphere awful, of making my J feel the need to build you up all the time. You're a *disgrace*."

Polly looked at me pleadingly.

"Why don't you go into the living room, Susanna? Come on, I'll be in in just a tick, with a cup of tea."

The doorbell rang all of a sudden, making all of us start. Everyone jolted slightly, as though no one had any idea as to how to react exactly. Wordlessly, I ran like the clappers towards the front door. Polly was hot on my heels. I swung the door open and to my surprise, saw Karen and Geoff standing there, shuffling about from foot to foot. They both looked the personification of uncomfortable.

"Hi, Susanna," Karen said, stammering a little.

"We were just passing by and we were just wondering if it would be okay if we called in for a little while?"

I didn't say a word but I stepped back and gestured for them to follow me inside. They scurried in, looking at Polly helplessly. I think that they were hoping I'd have slammed the door in their faces. They appeared stunned at having had their bluff called.

I led Polly, Karen and Geoff into the living room.

"How are you, Susanna?" Karen asked as she sat down tensely on the armchair.

"Jamie's still dead," I said flatly.

A strained silence descended upon the room.

Karen was evidently embarrassed.

"Stupid question, I'm sorry."

Geoff loosened his tie slightly. It had been tied so tightly it looked as though it was strangling him.

"We just wanted to check the arrangements for Wednesday," he said awkwardly.

"Yes, the funeral begins at half-past eleven," Polly said, leaping in quickly.

"Then afterwards, there will be a spread at the Fox and the Hound."

There was an excruciating silence.

"How are we with flowers?" Geoff mumbled.

"We're fine. Thanks, Geoff," Polly replied, looking agonised.

Karen appeared as though she was trying to pluck up the courage to ask something.

"Tell us if you'd prefer it just to be family flowers but Geoff and I would love to put together a wreath, from us and the kids. Everybody at your office wanted to organise one too, Susanna."

Geoff looked excited, as though he had something riveting to impart.

"I bumped into Dave earlier from the garage. He and the boys there wanted you to have a wreath from them…you know how much they valued Jamie. Dave was literally saying how he wasn't just a top mechanic, he was a top bloke."

They were all so *wrong*. It was time I set the record straight.

"The funeral most likely won't be taking place on Wednesday anyway, Geoff," I said. "Loads hasn't been done yet; it just wouldn't be possible."

Karen and Geoff looked confused. Polly looked sheepish.

"I've sorted it all, Susanna," she said in a small voice. "I didn't want to burden you with all of the logistics."

I sat there, the steely sense of bafflement I experienced seemed to be swamping me.

"We'd agreed that you'd sort out the Wake, you told me that. You said that you had the catering and everything all in hand. But you've not sorted out things like the coffin, have you?"

Polly looked humiliated, she stared down at her lap, wanting to evade eye contact.

"I just didn't want to put you in a position where you'd have to choose one," she said in a low voice.

This to me just beggared belief!

"Why on earth would you do that?" I demanded, the words escaping me in a clipped rush.

Polly squirmed in her seat; Karen and Geoff looked over at her pityingly. She'd certainly got their sympathy vote.

"I was trying to help, Susanna. You preferred me to speak with the police as you found it too upsetting hearing that Jamie's body was needed as evidence for quite some time. When I was told we could finally have the flipping funeral, I thought it would just be better for everyone if I just organised everything. I thought that you'd find it too raw, too painful."

I gasped as I got to my feet; feeling as though all the breath had been taken out of my body.

"Too *painful*? I struggle to remember a time when I wasn't engulfed by pain, Polly, because my boy is DEAD."

I began to stalk out of the room. I turned to face her, just before leaving.

"Thanks for that, I couldn't give a toss about which caterers you chose to make up a few sandwiches and a potato salad, but I *do* care that you couldn't even let me choose what my boy is going to rest in. You had to wade in as usual with your flipping size fives. All I'm going to see on Wednesday is the stuff that *you* picked. God, you really are a meddling little bitch."

Polly hid her head in her hands, as Karen and Geoff murmured soothingly to her. I stalked out into the kitchen. Adam nodded at me.

"All right, Mum?" he said, still holding the knife.

I glowered at the knife as though it was my nemesis.

"That, there, was used to end my baby's life," I said.

I didn't hang around to see Adam's reaction. I walked right out into the back garden, my face completely blank.

Two Days Later

I stood in the back garden, clutching a mug of tea that had long turned freezing. I watched the leaves blowing around the garden; they looked listless and disconnected, like they were in orbit. I could relate. I watched them; trying to numb my mind into thinking of anything other than the following day.

I heard someone come out into the garden behind me. I was expecting it to be Polly-put-the-kettle-on; poised to press yet more tea on me. I was shocked she'd not decided to simply force-feed me tea. There was time yet.

Adam presented himself at my side. He tapped me on the shoulder dubiously, as though I was a bad-tempered animal he wanted to keep at arm's length.

"Are you all right, Mum?" he asked. I think he was attempting to sound sincere and concerned. He enjoyed toying with me like this; pretending that he cared, pretending that there was some salvageability with him. There was nothing saveable about a nature like Adam's, he was incapable of ever becoming a genuine human being that could show consideration and nobility. No, taunting cat and mouse games would always be his style. I suppose I'd just grown tired of being his Stuart Little. I felt consumed with distaste, it was coming to something when I actually hoped that Polly would materialise at the kitchen window and call Adam in for some reason. It was ironic – normally I couldn't shake her off for two minutes and now when it would have actually suited me for her to have appeared, she was nowhere to be seen. *Typical.*

I tried to zone out but Adam was determined to not be ignored.

"Would you like a fresh tea?" he asked, nodding towards the mug I was holding.

"That one must be stone cold by now. You've been out here for an absolute age."

"I'm fine," I replied abruptly.

Go, go, go, go, go! I screamed silently inside my head.

He didn't. Unfortunately.

"I know how you're feeling, Mum," Adam said. He said it in such a way, that it sounded as though he was on the cusp of breaking into song. I would have found myself biting back laughter if I wasn't so nauseated by the comment he had just uttered.

"You don't know anything!" I snapped.

I physically turned away from him. I didn't want to have to keep looking at him. He wasn't giving up without a fight, he just ran around to face me again.

"I'm in the same boat as you," he said, stung.

"Tomorrow…"

Adam chewed his lip.

"Tomorrow's going to be really tough."

I looked at him fiercely. So fiercely, that he looked as though he was plotting his escape.

"A Maths exam is tough," I said shortly. "Losing touch with an old friend is tough. Losing my child, having to stand there in a stuffy, packed church tomorrow where I'll have to say goodbye to him for the last time…"

My chest felt like it was concaving; there was such intense pressure on it.

"That's not tough, that's soul-breaking!"

Adam bit his lip.

"I'm sorry, Mum, I should have chosen my words more carefully. But I just want you to know that *I'm* dreading tomorrow too. It's going to be awful and I don't want to stand here bullshitting you, pretending that it's all going to be fine. We're both probably going to want to cry and scream and shout all day because it's hardly going to be a picnic. But we have to be there for one another, we need to be able to fall back on each other."

He pretended to wipe his eyes, although it was obvious that there were no tears brimming there. I looked at him darkly.

"We need to try and give Jamie a send-off fit for a King," he said.

His tone was undeniably sour.

"It was what he deserved after all," he muttered bitterly.

I detested Adam.

"Jamie deserved to be alive!" I hissed venomously. I threw the mug of tea that I was clasping to the ground, the glass flying everywhere. The long-freezing tea splashed everywhere, including onto my bare feet. I blazed back into the house, damp and dismal and contemplated pouring myself a glass of water. I knew that was the drink I should be *having*. But it wasn't the drink that I *wanted.*

I poured myself a glass of water and threw it down the sink immediately after having poured myself it. I unscrewed the top of a bottle of wine, left sitting on the counter. I was surprised that Polly hadn't tipped the contents down the sink yet, but she clearly hadn't got around to it. I didn't bother getting a glass, I opted to drink straight from the bottle.

I felt overburdened with the oppressing knowledge of resigned misery.

Now

I was lying on the sofa in the living room. The curtains were drawn and I was surrounded by empty bottles. I'd been drinking heavily and my head was certainly paying the price for it. I lay there in a state of half-consciousness, wondering how strong my liver actually was. I was aware that I worked my way through a lot of wine a day. The off-license was the only reason that I left the house these days. I'd shuffle there at around 9 pm-ish when the streets were fairly quiet and it was unlikely that I'd run into anyone. I'd asked Polly at first to go on my behalf, but she refused. She had insisted on several occasions now that I was drinking myself to death and that she wasn't going to have any part to play in it. She said that she couldn't bear buying the substance that was slowly killing me and handing it over to me like it was no big deal. She always had to be awkward as difficult was her middle name. I hardly asked much of her – the one time I'd asked her for an exceedingly small favour and she'd turned me down! Typical Polly. She still religiously made me tea at half-hourly intervals. I wouldn't be surprised if it wound up that Polly was doing some sort of product placement deal with Twining's, as she really did seem to be tea-obsessed, with an omnipresent supply of teabags.

I'd gone to the off-license last night, to re-stock on supplies. The off-license isn't that far from my house, it's roughly a ten-minute walk. I left the house make-up free and bundled up in my big black coat, with my hood up to hide my face. I shuffled along the streets, not really looking at anyone properly. It was dark and I was banking upon that to shroud my identity. I so badly wanted to don an invisibility cloak so that I could simply go to the off-license; concealed and inconspicuous.

I knew I looked terrible. My hair resembled what could only be described politely as a *bird's nest* and my face was devoid of make-up, yet laden with wrinkles. It startled me how quickly I'd started to age. I looked dramatically older, by at least a decade or so. I wore dark tracksuit bottoms and a dark top to match. I looked the literal embodiment of, *the Woman in Black.* I could see people glancing curiously in my direction as I trailed along, looking like a little ghost. I felt like a ghost; lifeless and hopeless, with no prospects whatsoever.

I headed towards the off-license. I stopped for a second outside the shop, searching my purse for my credit card. I couldn't find it. I swore and grumbled to myself. I knew it had to be in there somewhere. I felt a surge of anger, I wouldn't have put it past that interfering shrew Polly to have pinched it! She'd trill that it was for my own good, at a later date. She really was a sanctimonious witch!

I rootled around desperately in my purse and to my utter joy; I discovered a crumpled twenty-pound note. Brilliant, Polly's hateful little plan had been foiled. Despite her best efforts to achieve the opposite outcome, I was going to get my drink. I was about to make my way into the off-license when Max came out. With Rachel. It all happened so fast that it was hard to know what I'd seen exactly, but I was fairly certain that they had been holding hands before they were aware, I was there. They sprang apart from each other, the second that they'd registered me.

Max was wearing his chunky polo-neck jumper that I'd given to him as a Christmas present last year. He looked muscled, his arms more defined. He looked as though he'd been larking around and laughing with Rachel before they both became aware of my presence. As for Rachel, her long blonde hair was serumed and straightened; her make-up was flawless and her posture was ramrod straight. She was clad in a clingy cream jumper, tight jeans and heeled boots. They both looked really…*good.* Happy. I couldn't quite believe my eyes. Jamie was barely dead and they were both just carrying on like everything was…normal. Despite the fact that it never would be. Ever again.

Rachel had the grace to look mortified. She mumbled an indistinctive hello and practically hid behind Max, leaving him to do all of the talking. I looked at her sceptically.

"Hey, Susanna!" Max said, enveloping me in a seamless hug.

"Rachel and I are heading back to Milstead for one night and one night only."

He paused, looking emotional.

"Everyone from our old school year is going back tonight to light some lanterns and remember Jamie. I think someone mentioned something about letting some balloons go too. Everyone's bringing food and drinks and things.

No one wants this to be a sad event, we're going to all treat it as a celebration of Jamie and who he was."

He quickly wiped a tear falling down the side of his face. Rachel had looked as though she was going to tenderly wipe it away for him; it was abundant that she was holding back, that she was filtering herself because I was there.

Max smiled at me bravely.

"Why don't you come down too, Susanna? Everyone would be so pleased to see you."

I shook my head. I could barely bring myself to speak.

Max nodded, as though he understood.

"Of course, no problem. If you happen to change your mind on the total off chance, everyone's planning on staying at Milstead until midnight and then we're all going to go back to Rachel's place. We—"

I couldn't bear to listen to any more of it. I brushed past Max, turning my back on him. I made my way into the shop. I could hear Max and Rachel speaking in hushed tones outside of the shop, evidently deliberating over whether to stay around outside, waiting for me. I can confirm that when I did emerge from the off-license ten minutes later, laden with two bulging bags, they were nowhere to be seen. They clearly hadn't cited me as warranting enough of a reason to be late for their piss-up. I felt so betrayed; so *angry*. Plus, Max and Rachel had never been close when Jamie was alive; not really. The only thing that they both really had in common was their mutual love for Jamie. Other than that, they didn't really share much common ground at all. Jamie had frequently fretted at the beginning of his romance with Rachel that he hated the thought of Max feeling left out, sidelined. Jamie never wanted Max to feel alienated, he was so keen for him and Rachel to be friends, to get along well together. However, it had always been relatively awkward. They had both tried their best for Jamie's sake, but it always felt like they were courteous acquaintances, at best. That seemed to have changed rather drastically now. They looked extremely *close* now.

I had run back to the house and threw myself onto the living room floor, lying there like a crumpled-up piece of paper and howling. Then, I'd methodically worked my way through every last bottle that I'd bought at the off-license.

Polly suddenly came into the room, she looked absolutely livid. She marched open and briskly pulled open the curtains. The sudden light was blinding. I covered my eyes with my arm and groaned.

"Drinking yourself into oblivion again, I see?" Polly said furiously.

She tapped at me impatiently.

"For heaven's sake, Susanna, it's barely midday. Can you not see that you've clearly got a problem?"

I waved her away dismissively. I was too tired to try and sugarcoat my intolerance of her. Polly sat down gingerly on the edge of the sofa. Her pinched face regarded me as though I was something that both looked and smelt very bad.

"Instead of drowning yourself in alcohol, you need to actually speak about what's coming up, Susanna," Polly said grimly.

I flailed at her; I was fed up with having to listen to her. I made an irritable sound and tried to make her leave me alone.

"Susanna, we *need* to discuss the trial," she said, her voice cracking.

"You need to talk about your feelings, as opposed to just trying to push them away for a short while with alcohol."

Who did she think she was? She was trying to sound like some sort of life coach. The only way someone like Polly could be a life coach would be if someone looked at her, listened to her drone on for an hour and thought at the end of the session. "Things may not be going so great for me at the moment. But at least I am not Polly – that is something."

I glared at Polly.

"Enough, enough. For the love of God, will you stop pecking my head? Why don't you just go to the kitchen and stick the kettle on? Do your thing."

I tried to roll away from her, but Polly stopped me from doing so.

"Susanna, for YOUR sake, I don't want you unable to remember a key event in your life because you're too boozed up to remember it."

She paused, looking sorrowful.

"Not again."

I felt like a seed of shame in the pit of my stomach had just been watered. It was growing and growing, I felt tormented by it. I couldn't think of it. I reached down and picked up a bottle of wine. It was getting to the stage where I felt I wasn't even tasting it anymore, as I drank it.

Polly scrolled through her phone urgently. I assumed she was probably on some website, trying to find out how she could stop me from drinking. She flashed the screen towards me.

"I saw this on Facebook this morning," she said.

"It was on Max's account, they all set off balloons at Milstead last night, to remember Jamie."

Polly showed me a flurry of photos of last night, posted by Max. There was one of Max and a couple of school friends, with their arms wrapped around each other. I noticed Rachel was in this photo. She and Max weren't beside each other, but she was staring up at him, her expression cryptic. Max was smiling for the camera, but it was evident that he was fighting every urge in his body to resist looking at her. There was something between them, a chemistry that the lens of the camera appeared to have captured with gut-wrenching accuracy. Both Max and Rachel suddenly resembled people with secrets.

I looked away from the screen and carried on drinking. I needed to *forget*.

Then

I lay on the sofa in the living room. The curtains were drawn but the sunlight was starting to seep its way into the room; trying to burningly weasel its way into my eyes. I couldn't stand it. I wanted complete darkness; I couldn't stand the daylight trickling its way into my space. My head was thumping, I reached out and touched my temples. My head felt as though it was about to burst.

My hair was still secured in the tight, unmoveable up do that it had been in since yesterday. I freed my hair and let it fall scraggily to my shoulders. At least it wasn't making my head pulse anymore, well, not to the same extent anyway. I'd caked on a load of makeup yesterday and I'd forgotten to take it off yesterday evening. It felt so heavy and restricting. I yawned. I could feel the makeup on my face starting to crack. I knew that I ought to wash it off upstairs first. Then I could come down again and lie on the sofa. I knew that was what I should do, but I just couldn't seem to bring myself to. I looked down at my clothes; my good black trousers, my black lace blouse. I didn't want to look at those clothes in the day, I couldn't face it. I shut my eyes. I kept my eyes clamped shut even when Polly came bursting into the room. I couldn't help but open my eyes just a fraction as she loomed over me to open the curtains. She looked devastated and contrastingly seething.

"Wake up, Susanna," she said briskly.

I lay there motionless, my eyes half-open. Polly's exasperation was so palpable, that she was practically vibrating.

"You should be ASHAMED, Susanna," Polly said. She was in tears.

"Being blotto at your own son's funeral – what on EARTH were you playing at?"

I didn't look at her, my face long and listless.

"Jamie deserved a respectful, peaceful funeral where everybody that held him dear, had the opportunity to say goodbye."

Polly's hands ball into fists.

"He did not deserve to have a day that should primarily have been about celebrating his life, being turned into a spectacle. I get that you're suffering immensely, Susanna, it's only natural that you want to lash out."

She shook her head; seething was an understatement.

"But rocking up as drunk as a skunk, practically HECKLING Adam when he was in the middle of making his beautiful eulogy, paying tribute to our darling J."

Polly rubbed her eyes, appearing increasingly riled as she recounts the events of yesterday.

"You were so rude to poor Rachel, Susanna. It was disgusting, you accusing her of being a slapper for hugging Max in a PLATONIC way. She was a mess; the poor lamb could barely put one foot in front of the other."

Polly practically hid her head in her hands.

"I wanted the flipping ground to swallow me up when you threw your bloody strop with poor Father McCabe. I couldn't believe it, you screeching at him like a banshee because he merely suggested that it might be a good idea for you to go to the Wake, as it might be something that you go on to regret otherwise."

Polly shook her head, looking anguished.

"He'd been great with you all morning Susanna; the man had the patience of a blooming saint. He was only being KIND to you and you ranted and raved at him like a madwoman."

I looked at Polly, dead in the eye.

"'Heaven needed another angel.' That's what he said," I uttered thickly.

Polly looked bewildered.

"That was a very sweet thing to say, Susanna. Why you were so up in arms about it is beyond me!"

"That platitude is just cruel," I said tightly.

"Heaven didn't need Jamie. But *I* do."

Polly sighed heavily.

"Jamie needed you to be at his Wake, Susanna," Polly said tiredly.

"He needed you to be his representative, he needed you to be amongst all of his nearest and dearest. Instead, you staggered back here and got blind drunk on your own."

She got such a kick out of trying to look down her nose at me. How dare she!

"I should have been at his wedding, his 30th birthday party, his children's birthday parties," I snapped.

Polly looked at me, almost pityingly as though I was missing the point altogether.

"You should have been there," she said simply as she left the room. I could hear her bustling around in the kitchen; chattering to Mr Jones. I heard the clicking sound of the kettle being switched on. Some things really did never change.

Tears slid down my face. I wiped them roughly with the back of my hand and picked up the bottle of wine. I looked at it for a moment; considering. Then I started glugging.

Now

I leaned over the sink; scrubbing at my face with a bar of soap that Polly had given to me. It smelt of her; all rosy and sickly, not the kind of scented soap I would ever have picked for myself in a million years. I resented my face even smelling of a scent that she'd picked out but I knew that I needed to wash my face very, very badly. My skin had started to feel so dry and itchy and Polly had whined on about me ending up with dermatitis if I wasn't careful, maybe even some nasty skin condition. She had said this to me with a slight smirk on her face as if she got a thrill out of seeing me panic. I couldn't give a stuff about nasty skin conditions but I was starting to reach the conclusion myself that my face could do with a wash. I'd long since run out of the cleanser that I had always used religiously before Jamie's death. Polly had promised to nip out and get some, but she hadn't done so yet. She'd handed me over her silly cake of rosy soap as though she was bestowing a wondrous gift upon me. I think she had genuinely expected me to be *grateful*, to practically bow down and kiss her feet. She could whistle!

Polly had hovered uncertainly for a minute or two when I'd first started rubbing at my face with the soap. I'd stared at her hard in the mirror until even she took the hint to beetle off and to give me two minutes of privacy. I frequently felt like a zoo animal these days; constantly gawped at, my audience always looking at me with curious fascination as though they couldn't wait to see what I was going to do or say next. It was very exhausting.

I conceded that my face had been washed well enough when I practically couldn't see my face beneath its mask of soaped-up lather. A little soap had managed to worm its way into my left eye. It stung like crazy; I blinked rapidly to try and get it out. I remembered that Jamie used to think absolutely nothing of falling over and grazing himself when he was a little boy, but he used to shriek in agony if he ever got any shampoo in his eyes, when I was washing his hair for him when he was small. Even as an adult, Jamie used to joke that those kiddie shampoos that claimed to induce *no tears*, needed to be pulled from the shelves. He said that he had no clue what was in those bottles, but that whatever it was that they contained, it hurt like hell.

I leaned over the sink and started splashing water onto my eye wildly, in the hope that I'd be able to wash away the soap. I started furiously splashing water up onto my face. As the water splashed up, it was as though I was confronted with memories from the past. Not of Jamie. Of his *funeral*.

Despite having done my level best to try and blot out Jamie's funeral, the memories were staring me in the face; insistent and unbearable. I splashed water on my face harder, in a bid to try and prevent myself from having to be faced with those memories, when I didn't want to remember them. I didn't; I didn't; I didn't.

No such luck. It didn't look as though I had any real choice in the matter.

I was back there at the funeral. I kept trying to tell myself that I wasn't; it was my imagination, this was only a memory. Part of the past, not my present. But it felt so real, so cuttingly raw. I saw Adam standing near the altar, facing the congregation. The vast majority of which were crying dismally, Jamie's friends looking unrecognisable in clinical black clothes, that just seemed so wrong, somehow. Rachel was sitting very near the front, her shoulder pressed into Max's shoulder as though it was all too much for her to be there. She was clearly finding it difficult to cope; the funeral couldn't end fast enough as far as she could see.

Adam cleared his throat slightly before speaking. He spoke about a stranger, "Dearest, James" whom he had been inseparable with; they were forever bouncing off each other, larking around, driving their poor old mum potty. The congregation tittered at this in the false, forced way that people do at funerals when someone has a bash at humour in their eulogy. I sat there; disarmed with disbelief. I couldn't believe that someone could go up and try and take centre-stage at a funeral, as they outright lied through their teeth, making a eulogy. Adam spoke about all the times he and *dearest* James had gotten up to mischief together. They were always in each other's pockets. I sat there; hardly able to contain sarcastic laughter. I had fought every single instinct to turn around and scream at the top of my lungs to the congregation, "Please tell me that no one is actually buying this drivel! Jamie and Adam were no closer than the man on the flipping moon and it is an insult for him to be standing up there, simpering about him as though they were joined at the hip, when the bottom line is, he was an utter wretch to him when he was alive and he couldn't stand to see the joy in his nature!"

I didn't. I managed to fight the urge to yell this to anyone that would listen to me. My head was hurting, I remembered that my updo felt far too stiff and far too restricting. Polly had practically drowned my head in hairspray to keep it rigid and unmoving and had fastened down any loose strands with hairpins. I had caught a glimpse of myself before leaving the house and had worried terribly that it looked as though my sadistic shrew of a sister had styled my hair in a mohawk. Great, I was turning up at my own son's funeral, resembling Sonic the fucking Hedgehog.

Adam remained at the front, enjoying the close attention. Formerly, he would never have been in a position where he had masses sitting before him, all listening intently to the words that came out of his heinous mouth. Adam regaled some fictitious tall tales about him and Jamie, he was trying to imply that they were the familial equivalent of Ant and Dec, for crying out loud. Then he locked eyes with me; he smirked, looking strangely aroused by all of the angst that he saw on the pews before him. Then he turned around and slammed down his Ace card.

"I think Jamie's death has taught us that life really is short. I think that with this in mind, looking around the room today, at all of the people who are here to pay their respects to Jamie, I think it would be good if everyone could leave today, vowing to be a bit kinder, a bit nicer, a bit better. We all know what happened to Jamie but I don't want anyone to focus on how his life was taken away from him. I want it to be a case that we all think about how we can carry Jamie's legacy on- to coin Oasis, 'don't look back in anger'. In a world where we can be and do anything, let's be kind."

There was applause. There was actual applause from the congregation. At Jamie's *funeral.* Karen stood up and clapped uproariously, as though he'd just won an Oscar and she was celebrating his success from her table. I couldn't believe it. Polly, who was sitting beside me, in a skirt far too short for the occasion and heels that made her resemble a call-girl, looked at me and whispered, "Oh Susanna, he was incredible. Aren't you *proud*?"

This was the final straw for me. I couldn't bear it. I couldn't stand to sit there and to be a part of Adam's forked-tongued façade for a second longer. I stood up, wobbling slightly because I had had to have a few glasses of wine before leaving the house that morning, knowing it was going to be a hellish day. I'd screeched at Adam. I'd called him despicable and depraved for trying to deface Jamie's memory. He'd tried to take ownership of him when he was dead because he knew that the real truth didn't reflect the kind of anecdotes that you'd reel off about someone at a funeral. I had blazed at him for having the sickening audacity to stand there in front of everybody, for singing Jamie's praises when he'd always done his utmost to make his home life a total misery. I had blasted him for being a hideous freak that looked visibly as though his own engines were revving at his brother's funeral. I'd reached out to hit him, but Polly had pulled me back down to my seat; hissing at me to stop showing myself up.

"You're making yourself look a complete idiot," she wailed in a whisper. "Stop embarrassing me!"

I couldn't believe that she had the nerve to suggest that she felt I was an embarrassment to her. I looked at her; she had so much make-up on that she looked like a ruddy drag queen, her skirt resembled a belt and she was tottering around in stilettos at my son's funeral. I glanced at the shoes. They were my shoes, the ones that Karen had given to me the previous Christmas. She'd clearly taken it upon herself to purloin them from my bedroom, without so much as asking first. She was acting as though we were teenagers again; her swiping things from my wardrobe so she'd look as good as possible at whatever House Party it was that she was frequenting that weekend. She had spent an age beautifying herself this morning; she had acted as though my child's funeral was London Fashion Week. It was sending me spare that she was even sitting beside me on the front pew and that she had the cheek to sit there without one iota of embarrassment. She was never exactly going to take the mantel for Aunt of the Year, yet she still sat there sombrely, as though she was the picture of the grieving Aunt, mourning her beloved nephew. The hypocrisy was hateful!

I had ended up snarling at Polly, pretty loudly actually. I'd lost my temper when everyone had been warbling, *The Lord's my Shepherd*. I'd told her she was a repellent, grisly little rodent that needed to scuttle off back to her own sewer and out of my face. I could see Max in the corner of my eye, looking at me worriedly, his face the picture of concern. I felt momentarily relieved, at least there was someone in this congregation that genuinely cared about me.

I turned around to look at him, only to see Rachel clinging to him. Her hair was scraped back in an austere ballerina bun. It looked as though she had a satellite stuck to her head. Her lipstick was too bright and her eyelashes were so laden with mascara, that it looked as though spiders-legs were growing out of her face. She was visibly shaking and she was turning an alarming shade of green, as though she was on the cusp of being sick. Her hands were on Max's broad chest, her face was millimetres away from his as she whispered something to him that I couldn't quite catch. Max leaned down to her, he whispered something tenderly in her ear. She nodded, clinging tighter all the while. There was something so unsettlingly intimate about the gesture. I couldn't believe that Rachel would be all-over Jamie's best friend like a cheap suit, on the day of his funeral! She really was something else; she'd shown her true colours.

I'd erupted at her, I'd blasted Rachel for being such a cheap tart, for trying to get her paws on the first man with a pulse that showed her kindness. I had screamed at her that she had never deserved Jamie and that she had the cheek of Nelson for daring to show her face that day, when she should have been off, hanging her horrid little head in shame somewhere. Max had looked at me; his features overcome with disappointment. He'd looked at me as though I was some sort of monstress, exploding at poor little Rachel for no valid reason at all. Rachel bawled and shook, but I was relentless. I shouted at her to stop playing the victim, she wasn't pulling the wool over my eyes, I had her card marked. I could see Tilly, further along the pew. She looked about ten, with her long pale hair pushed back by a mauve Alice band. She couldn't meet my gaze when she reached across and patted Rachel's shoulder comfortingly. The same Rachel that had teased her rottenly when they were back at school, the same Rachel that was the covert ringleader of all the catty girl gangs that made Tilly's school days as bleak as possible. I had to turn away, I couldn't stand to look at them anymore.

When the funeral ended, I'd staggered out of the church. I wasn't going to go to the Wake, I couldn't abide being around all of these people who'd pour me tea and offer me platitudes with a feeble smile, or who would regard me as though I was an incoming cyclone, that they'd keep a distance from at all times and who wouldn't look me in the eye as they uttered a brief hello.

Polly scurried down the aisle after me, wheedling with me to go to the Wake. I'd told her to get out of my face, I'd made it plain what my plans were and that she didn't have a right to be telling me what to do. Polly had insisted upon Father McCabe having a chat with me outside of the church. Father McCabe gave me the creeps, he resembled a daddy-long-legs and he always emitted a discharged energy that meant you never really felt relaxed in his presence. He had two ginger tufts of hair stuck to his head that alarmingly resembled the fur balls that Karen's cat Garfield produced. We'd always joked that Father McCabe had nicked them and had opted to stick them to his head. He'd come up to me; patronising and poisonous. He'd licked his lips malevolently when he'd spoken about what a fine, young man Jamie had been. I'd slapped at him when he insisted on spouting that "Heaven had needed another angel". Polly had actually had to intervene; she'd had to yank me away from Father McCreep because I was giving unbeknown to me, Anthony Joshua a run for his money, with the pounding I gave to his wiry chest.

I felt shaken. I turned off the tap; I stopped and tried to control my breathing which had become scarily shallow. I roughly dried my face with a towel and stumbled out of the bathroom. Polly was loitering on the landing, looking reticent. She'd clearly been hanging around for quite some time now.

"Susanna, how about we do something today?" she suggested all of a sudden.

I stared at her blankly.

"It's really important that you get out of the house. You don't want to just be holed up in here twenty-four hours a day. It's no wonder that you're getting…"

She paused.

"Depressed."

I found myself flinching, as though I'd been scalded. Polly winced, looking guilty.

"Let's go out, walk to a coffee shop," she said gently.

"You don't have to talk, not if you don't want to. All you have to do is to sit there, out in public, for a little while. Could you do that for me, Susanna?" she asked.

She tried to smile, but it looked as though she was on the verge of tears.

"Come on, do it for me. I'm gasping for a cappuccino. Instant's just not cutting it for me anymore."

I pulled at my hair listlessly.

"I was going to look through old photos," I said hoarsely.

"You can do that later," Polly pointed out.

"It doesn't have to be an either-or situation. You can do that later on, for as long as you want. But *please* do this for me, Susanna. Just this one thing, come on, I've hardly asked much of you, have I?"

I stared at her steadily.

"Fine," I replied monosyllabically.

Later That Day

I walked along the street beside Polly. She burbled and blethered relentlessly for the first few minutes. I didn't utter a word in response. It seemed that at long last; she took the hint that I didn't feel in the mood to be chirping about the weather and she gradually became silent too.

I was aware that I looked in a complete state. I trudged along; staring at the ground as I couldn't stand the thought of looking at anyone. I couldn't abide the thought of seeing anyone that I knew, of seeing their faces crease up with pity; looking at me with the patronising head-tilt as they parroted some platitude about grief that they had probably read on a mug somewhere. I wanted to crunch up small and I made a point out of hunching so much that I probably resembled a hunchback. My hair looked woeful; it fell scraggily past my shoulders in greasy wisps. I was barefaced and I was aware that my face bore an alarming grey complexion. I trailed along, in my oldest jeans and big baggy jumper that I'd been considering donating to the hospice shop. I'd always found it way too baggy but I was glad of that now, it swamped me. I felt immersed and cocooned in it. I badly hoped that it would serve in making me largely invisible to people. I loathed the thought of being conspicuous.

I glanced over at Polly fleetingly. She, on the other hand, looked the picture of contentment. Her face was fully adorned with make-up, her hair was newly washed and styled. She walked tall, shoulders back, clacking along like a pony in her heeled thigh-high boots. It looked as though she had obviously sent off for a new coat at some point too, as she was clad in a new pea coat, noticeable in her duck-egg blue. Polly looked as though she didn't have a care in the world. She smiled at passers-by; she grinned suggestively at men driving by in cars. It didn't matter what tragedy had happened in the family, Polly was forever on the prowl.

I heard Polly take a sharp intake of breath, as we rounded the next corner. We both knew what was coming.

"Are you alright, Susanna?" she asked me shrilly, whilst making no effort to actually look at me. I made no attempt to reply.

I looked at the garage on the right. *Jamie's* garage. He'd loved working there. He used to lark around singing, "Greased Lightning" and capering about, making everyone hoot with laughter. Jamie was the life and soul; he had always been a natural entertainer, a true showman. Jamie would sometimes forget his lunch and I'd receive an urgent text message later in the day, asking me if I could be a total lifesaver and bring it around for him. I used to always feel my heart swell with pride at arriving with Jamie's sandwiches later, to see him parading about, laughing and singing, his jauntiness and joviality infectious.

I didn't want to look at the garage. Jamie wasn't going to be there; it wasn't the same. I wanted to walk right past it, avoid it at all costs.

No such luck.

Dave and Kev were standing outside the garage, drinking coffee. They looked deep in conversation. Dave was a small, stocky man in his early thirties, whereas Kev was a tall, blond man roughly around my own age. He'd dated Karen years earlier, funnily enough; he was her last boyfriend before she met Geoff and she wound up marrying him. Dave suddenly glanced over – he'd spotted me. He whispered something pressingly to Kev and then they both came pounding up, clearly wanting to say something. They both looked visibly shocked to see me and they'd hurtled over so fast, that they nearly dove straight into Polly.

"Susanna, love, I'm so glad that I've seen you!" Dave said urgently.

"I wanted to talk to you at the funeral but…"

There was an excruciating pause. Dave was trying to spare my blushes – he didn't want to admit that we'd not spoken at Jamie's funeral because I had been bladdered.

"But I just didn't get a chance, really," he said quickly, relieved to have concocted some kind of excuse.

"I just wanted to say what an amazing bloke Jamie was," Dave continued. "Life and soul, he really was. The place just isn't the same. Dead quiet."

He winced at his word choice.

"Sorry, sorry, I've never had a way with words."

Kev patted Dave on the shoulder consolingly.

"It's so *quiet* without him. He was always making us laugh. There was always some story he had to tell, some joke. He was a one-off."

I felt deadened. Polly went to take my hand but I recoiled from the gesture. She was evidently embarrassed but she cleared her throat and tried to masquerade her humiliation by engaging in conversation with them.

"Thanks, Dave, Kev. Jamie, he loved working here. I know that you were like The Three Musketeers, you all got on like a house on fire."

Dave looked reticent before saying shyly, "We'd like to be there, at the trial. If that's okay. We're all in Jamie's corner. That bloke, that *waster* is going to see that he picked on the wrong lad. Jamie was loved by the masses and that freak of nature's going to have that rammed home."

I couldn't listen to it anymore. I abruptly walked on; feeling colour rise to my cheeks as I bolted down the street. Polly practically had to jog to keep up with me.

"They're trying, Susanna," she said breathlessly. "They just wanted to be supportive. And they're right. Jamie was adored and that is exactly what that killer is going to see."

I chewed my lip. I felt hollow with pain. I didn't want to be out; I wanted to be back at home, looking through all of my old photos of Jamie. I needed to feel close to him; I felt so set adrift being out and about now. It was like being lost in a dark, deserted forest with no hope and nobody to turn to.

I couldn't stand it. Especially given what I knew was coming up on my left. There is nothing more unthinkable than walking along your child's memory lane when you know that they're never going to create any new ones. This was it – this was all I had. I felt on the cusp of tears; I went to turn on my heel to return home but Polly was steering me with insistence. She was leading me forwards. I knew that she wanted eye contact. She wanted me to talk to her but I couldn't think of anything worse.

I saw the back entrance to Milstead comprehensive; Jamie's old secondary school. Polly pointed at the gate – it was as though she wanted to torture me. Did she honestly think I wouldn't remember where the flaming school was, that I wouldn't feel oppressed with memories of Jamie from the past that seemed so tantalisingly close, yet so devastatingly out of reach?

"I remember Jamie always used to be getting told off for leaping over that gate when leaving school in the afternoons," Polly said wryly, as she looked reflectively over the road. She laughed slightly, although it emerged as more of a choked sound.

"The school was so prickly about people jumping over that gate, but no one could ever stay cross at Jamie for long. He was so charming, that they could only pretend to be irked for about two minutes, before ruffling his hair and sending him on his way. He could sweet-talk the birds out of the trees; that lad. He could wriggle his way out of anything."

It astounded me that she could actually show such a lack of sensitivity. I glared at her before uttering dryly, "Oh yes, life was such a breeze for Jamie. He could charm the socks off anyone. It's a shame that that killer couldn't be sweet-talked, isn't it?"

Polly looked defeated. She didn't say a word until we reached a small coffee shop on the corner of the street. I hadn't been to it in a long while, I remembered Karen and I used to come here all the time when Jamie and Tilly were both little.

I felt overwhelmed by the smell of steamed milk as I shuffled in the door, after Polly. The lights felt so overpoweringly bright. A woman at a table in the centre of the coffee shop was talking so loudly that I felt as though my ears were hurting. She was talking so loudly that she was practically yelling at the perplexed woman opposite her, she sprayed coffee cake crumbs disgustingly as she pontificated. I felt sick.

"You take a seat, Susanna," Polly told me gently. "Find a table and I'll bring the drinks over."

I felt as though I was in a daze. I dragged myself over to the one remaining table left unoccupied in the coffee shop. Unfortunately, it was situated right by the window. Which was fine for someone who liked people watching and didn't flinch at the thought of public scrutiny. Someone that wasn't me.

I sat down self-consciously. I felt as though everyone in the coffee shop was staring at me. The grief-stricken Mother on tour. I knew that they were all waiting with bated breath to see if I'd suddenly start sobbing and shaking; the picture of melancholic misery or, if I'd sit and snaffle a slice of Red Velvet cake and babble on about some sort of Netflix series; desperate to speak about anything other than what had happened. I hated their stares; their gall, the holier-than-thou expressions that they wore whenever I shuffled past them. I privately suspected that they could smell the booze. I didn't exactly prioritise washing these days and I knew myself that I had been drinking far too much recently.

It seemed like a lifetime ago that I sat in this coffee shop with Karen; kids plonked on our laps as we enjoyed a long girly gossip. It all just seemed so superficial; so shallow now. Why did I waste precious time that could have been spent on Jamie, on moaning about why we still couldn't squeeze into our best jeans and rabbiting on about how we'd share a slice of Victoria sponge so we didn't feel bad about it later, with Karen? I felt so angry with myself; annoyed beyond words. I'd not utilised the time I'd had with Jamie and I knew that guilt and self-irritation couldn't turn back the clock, no matter how much I wanted it to.

I sat hunched and haunted, vowing to inhale whatever it was that Polly had ordered for me. The sooner I'd finished, the sooner I could get out of here and get home. I could look through all of Jamie's photographs, I could will him alive, even if it was just in my head. If only I could try hard enough and not be interrupted, I was sure that I could do it. I was sure…

"Susanna!" a voice suddenly said from behind me.

I turned around gingerly, to see Maggie from work. She was wearing a scarf that made her look like a French waiter, with a string of onions wound around her neck, and her hair was pinned back in an elaborate French twist. She oozed patronising pity.

"Oh Susanna, you poor love, it's so good to see you out and about! I wanted to call you countless times, I picked up the phone hundreds of times but I just couldn't bring myself to press call."

Maggie pretended to give herself a rap on the wrists, as though she was taking part in some sort of one-woman Punch and Judy show.

"I just kept thinking to myself, 'Maggie, you're a daft old mare that has a habit of making a dog's dinner of things when it comes to sensitive issues!'. You know me, I always try and make a bit of a joke out of things."

She tapped my arm fondly.

"The office just hasn't been the same," she said, as though I'd been signed off work for a week with the flu.

"We've all been thinking away about you and Adam, of course. How's he doing, the little chicken?"

I didn't reply. The whole situation was torturous. Maggie's tactlessness and self-involvement was borderline breath taking. I could see Polly looking anxiously over at me from the till. Despite having not imparted a single word to her, Maggie ploughed on regardless.

"The trial's around the corner. I don't know how you can *function.* If it was my Rory, I just don't think I'd cope."

I couldn't take it for a second longer.

I sprang to my feet and flew past a befuddled Maggie to the door. Polly called desperately after me, pleading with me to stay. I didn't listen to her.

I ran out of the door and sprinted down the road; needing to get far away. I pounded down the streets; the tears that I'd been holding in throughout that spectacle, pouring down my face. My lank hair billowed behind me as I moved. I was aware of familiar faces, of voices mumbling about how they were thinking of me; they'd light a candle for J on the day of the trial, he'd never be forgotten. I didn't stop with anyone. I didn't even stop to listen properly. My feet were starting to throb and my chest was starting to tighten with breathlessness. I wheezed and gasped, but I knew that I had to keep on running.

I felt tormented, I was consumed briefly with memories of Jamie from the past but that awful memory, the one of him murdered and maimed, no matter how much the undertakers had tried to conceal the worst of the damage, was the one that kept squirming its way into my thoughts; gut-wrenchingly real.

I tried to run away from those thoughts, I ran until I physically couldn't any longer. I stopped for breath outside an Old People's Home. I cried harder.

Then

I sat on a hard plastic chair in a communal sitting room, beside Polly; opposite a baffled-looking elderly woman. It looked as though someone had put ten pence in her when I wasn't looking; she was in overdrive, burbling and babbling. I couldn't subject myself to listen to the specific words coming out of her mouth, but I could just hear manic cheeriness. It was like being at Disneyland at 2 pm in a queue of screaming children in forty-degree heat. All of the parents wearily placating their offspring as they donned Mickey Mouse headbands and tried to reassure their brood that there was no reason to be pouting or crying, as *we were all supposed to be having fun.* That's what Polly reminded me of now. Except she never would have gone the whole way to Orlando with two young children. She'd have probably gone on her own, partied the week away as she cosied up to an unsuitable man. She'd then regale Fifty Shades-style tall tales when she'd return to England, boasting about how the Americans truly appreciated her, she may as well pack up and move to the States for good. She truly was a joke.

Polly was trying hard to engage with the puzzled old woman before us. She was talking very loudly, so loudly that some of the carers were starting to peer over curiously in our direction. Polly didn't seem to mind, if anything she just got louder. She seemed to think that shouting her words as opposed to saying them in a normal tone of voice would make this frail old lady suddenly have a *Eureka* moment if you will, where she'd suddenly snap back to normal and witter on to Polly as though she was who she had been as opposed to how she was now.

I never thought I'd see a day where I'd be sitting across from my dear old mum and feeling so little. It had broken my heart when she was diagnosed with Alzheimer's two years previously. I found it astounding to think that there had once been a time when my mother's condition had been such a source of pain to me; it seemed inconceivable to me now. I remembered vividly the first time that she had forgotten who I was. I knew that she couldn't help it, she'd not *chosen* to have this cruel disease. I was aware that I needed to not take her confusion to heart, but it had always felt like such a *rejection* when she'd forgotten who I was. Alzheimer's was ruthless, it slowly snatched your loved one away, bit by bit, to a point where they were hardly recognisable. To an extent where you felt as though you were sitting opposite a stranger, as much as your elderly loved one looked at you too, as though they had never clapped eyes on you in their life. I found it unbelievable to think that there had once been a time when my mother's condition has given me sleepless nights, as I'd tossed and turned, fretting about what the future had in store for her. Now, I hardly cared that she sat across from me, a look of courteous detachment on her face. As far as my mother was concerned, Polly and I are no more significant to her than the tea lady that bustles by every few minutes, offering tea that resembles a peculiar orange colour and own-brand Jammy Dodger biscuits.

I couldn't stand Jammy Dodger biscuits. I think I associated them with Dean. He used to eat mountains of them on a daily basis; hoovering up a whole packet with a single cup of tea that he'd slurp noisily as he'd watch daytime telly. This was when the building site had let him go. I remembered that there was a two-year period where he'd sit pyjamaed and peeved in the living room; wallowing and wasting. I remembered encouraging him to be proactive, to have a shower and smarten himself up. I'd told him umpteen times that he needed some fire in his belly. He couldn't expect a job to simply be plonked into his lap. That was the thing with Dean though, all of his get-up-and-go had seemingly got up-and-gone. Well, until he really upped and left with his dolly bird. But that was beside the point.

Dean had actually called me before I'd left the house to come to the nursing home with Polly. It had been extremely uncomfortable, we'd not exactly finished on bad terms, but as much as we were still largely capable of civilities, for the most part, we'd never really had a major reason to speak. I couldn't really see why he'd decided it was a good idea to ring. He'd called the landline as opposed to my mobile, which I had found to be somewhat strange. He'd probably hoped that someone else would pick up. He'd have felt off the hook then, he'd attempted to phone me but he hadn't been able to get through. I bet he'd been silently praying that Polly or even Adam would pick up. No such luck, he got me. Dean had mumbled that he was really sorry about what had happened. Jamie was a top-tier person, he couldn't believe it. He tried to reminisce about Jamie, and he spoke to me about memories from the past. I was even a little receptive to begin with, surprising myself. Dean apologised again for having not been able to attend the funeral. He lived in Manchester these days with his new girlfriend; he had a young family with her. He wouldn't have been able to pack up for days on end, to leave her on her own with the boys. He sounded genuinely sorry; I told him that it was fine; I understood. The conversation had been going okay. But then Dean had to wade in with his size tens and ruin it.

"Everything that's happened, it's all such a waste, isn't it?" he'd said earlier, exclaiming in an uncharacteristically animated way.

I misunderstood and assumed that he meant that the killer was a waste, that's what I presumed Dean had been trying to say.

No.

"I just meant that Jamie's life just seems such a waste-to have all those prospects, only to be slain to death in a bar. It's just terrible."

I had been furious; I had blazed at Dean for daring to call Jamie a *waste*. It was such an ugly word, tarring and twisted. I'd unleashed at Dean down the phone. I'd called him every name under the sun and had made no secret of my revulsion for him. His stupid girlfriend came on to the phone then. Dean had obviously opted to hide behind her skirt. She'd been sickly sweet with me at first, trying to insinuate that butter wouldn't melt in her mouth. I'd roared at her, screeching that she needed to mind her own and to put that lummox of a man of hers back on to the line as I had plenty more to say to him. Well, I said it in much more colourful language than that, but I'm sure that you get the gist. She had got quite heated then, shouting some awful things at me. She had accused me of being a drunkard. I said some pretty horrendous things about how she'd better watch out that her two sprogs don't end up like Adam. She'd slammed the phone down.

The tea lady tried to waft yet another cup of tea under my nose. I felt like I was going stir-crazy. What was it with people trying to constantly ply me with tea? I felt as though I'd go bananas if I ever had to look at the stuff again.

"Hello, dear," my mum said suddenly.

I looked at her, fleetingly puzzled. I wondered in a half-beat if for a split-second she remembered me?

"It's nice to meet you," my mum continued. "My name's Alison."

She didn't have a clue who I was. Polly's shoulders sunk slightly; I think she'd been hoping for some sort of Disney moment. However, this was real life, plain and simple and the bottom line is that my mum doesn't have the faintest idea as to who I am and there's nothing that can be done to change that.

I felt so removed, I just found it unthinkable to reflect on all of the occasions that I'd shed countless tears at the kitchen table as I spent hours upon hours researching every scrap of information about Alzheimer's available on the Internet. Now, I found it impossible to lament over my mother's inevitable deterioration and ultimate demise. My mum had always led a very full and happy life; she'd married her childhood sweetheart (my dad) and they'd been married for a fantastic fifty years, before his death. They had always been very much in love and their closeness had always been so heartening to see. Every Saturday morning, my parents used to go to the local garden centre which was only a short drive from their house. They'd go and mooch around; pick a new plant every week and wrap up their visit with a trip to the café, where they'd enjoy a cream tea. This had been their routine for as long as I could remember. When my father died fourteen years previously, I had known that my mum had sorely missed her Saturday jaunts with my dad. I had tried to take her to the garden centre instead, except I had to bring along Jamie and Adam so it was a very different dynamic for my mum. Jamie was as good as gold, he had such a soft spot for his grandmother and she openly adored him. Jamie sat beautifully with his gingerbread man in the café, he enjoyed looking around the shop, smelling all of the different plants. Adam used to wrench my fingers right back whenever I held on to his hand, he'd screech demandingly if he didn't get the toy he wanted in the shop, he would wail dismally if he didn't get two cakes in the café. We had all persevered and had tried to make these jaunts as a foursome a more regular occurrence but after about six visits, my mum privately confided to me that she liked to think of the garden centre as her and my dad's place, so maybe if we were all going out, we could go somewhere different instead.

I always remembered my mum's reaction when Jamie was born. I always smiled when I thought about the joy that both she and my dad had felt. They were literally walking on the clouds. I remembered my mum holding a newborn Jamie close to her as she confessed to me softly, "You and Polly always meant the absolute world to me and I was so happy to have two delightful daughters. But truth be told, I had always secretly wanted a son as well."

She had looked at Jamie so wistfully and had said so lovingly, "I really am elated for you, Susanna. James is a *beauty*. He really is a little treasure."

My mum was so happy to finally have a bouncing baby boy in the family. She loved taking Jamie for long walks in his pram; she smiled proudly whenever anyone came up to ooh and coo over him.

“He’s just filled a void in our lives that we never even knew existed. He has completed our family, in a way, we just never would have thought possible.”

I’d known that my mum was wracked with worry at how I was going to cope with looking after Jamie, without Tom around. However, she was quickly reassured. She knew that it just worked. Jamie became my whole world overnight and everything revolved around him. My mum wanted to come around all of the time to help take care of him. I rarely asked her but she just loved Jamie so much, that she missed him hugely whenever he wasn’t around.

I felt a temporary pang of guilt for feeling so little towards my mum when we had always had a good relationship. Jamie and her had had such a special bond, he was the apple of her eye. She had always lit up whenever he came into the room. But I just couldn’t shake off the fact that it should have been her funeral that I had been attending, not Jamie’s. I would have been upset at my mum’s funeral, of course, I would have been. It would have been emotional, no doubt about it but I would have found it sobering to have the knowledge that my mum had led a plentiful life, her experiences rich and vast. She’d had two children; two grandchildren.

Whereas Jamie’s life had barely begun, he was only twenty-one! I was detached once more.

“My name’s Polly.” Polly blethered to my mother. “I’m your oldest daughter.”

She pointed briefly at me before continuing airily, “This is Susanna, she’s your youngest daughter.”

My mum looked angry.

“Do you think I’m daft? I’m not over the hill just yet, I’ll have you know. “

She shook her head, looking perturbed.

“Honestly, I don’t have two daughters. I have a son.”

Polly looked perplexed.

“You’re getting a little bit mixed up there, Mum. You did say that you always had a feeling that I was going to be a boy when you were pregnant with me. You told me that you and Dad had picked the name Henry out if I had been a boy. Do you remember that, Mum? Do you remember?”

My mum shook her head at Polly impatiently.

“I have a son, a beautiful son. I want to see him,” she said adamantly.

I rolled my eyes. I looked longingly at the clock, wondering when I could escape.

"Sorry, I'm such a drag to be around," snapped my mum. "You just wait, your jaw's going to hit the floor when my son comes in. He's the best young man that you could ever wish to set eyes on. His name's James."

I stiffened. My mum had never called James, Jamie. She'd always said that James was too lovely a name to abbreviate and that he'd always be James to her.

"He's a wonderful lad," my mum continued warmly.

"He always visits me, he brings me cakes, tells me about all of his escapades. He'll probably be here soon. Then you two can see him for yourselves…"

I shook, feeling as though I was in searing pain. Polly looked emotional.

"James wasn't your son, Mum, he was Susanna's. He was your grandson."

My mum waved her away.

"Whatever, whatever. He'll be here, soon enough. "

I doubled over at the waist in my seat. It was as though I'd just been kicked hard in the stomach, over and over again.

Polly tucked a piece of hair behind an ear and leaned forward so that she was closer to Mum.

"I've told you this time and time again, Mum. It's shocking and it's unfair but…"

She took a long, laboured breath.

"James isn't here anymore. He's dead."

My Mum made a low, moaning sound like an animal in significant pain before building up into a scream.

"No, you're a liar! You're both vicious liars! He's not dead, he's here, he's here! James! *James*!"

I leapt to my feet and charged out of the room. I was aware of tears pouring down my face as I raced out of the nursing home. Memories of Jamie from babyhood to adulthood stormed through my mind; invasive and constant. I experienced the memories so intensely that it was to a throwing extent. It was as though I was being pushed toward the sign, welcoming people to, *Sunnyside Nursing Home*. Then the memory I was haunted by, Jamie attacked and gaping, lying there on a slab. I screeched as I slapped at my own head violently, trying to beat the memory out of my head. Polly appeared; she was crying too. She tried to take my hand, but I shoved her away furiously.

"Don't you ever make me do that again!" I erupted at her.

"Our mother has Alzheimer's, of course, she's not going to remember that Jamie is dead. You should have just come on your own like you had been doing since everything that's happened, happened. It was warped, making me be there as she's told."

Polly looked at me; her bottom lip wobbling.

"Susanna, I'm sorry, I really am sorry. Come here…"

She attempted to hug me but I elbowed her away.

"Fuck off, Polly, get out of my sight," I snapped as I stalked off in the direction of the High Street.

Polly called after me shrilly, wanting to know where I was going. She thought it was best that I didn't take myself off on my own if I was feeling so upset.

This seemed ludicrous, I was never going to not be upset now. It was as simple as that. I swore at her bitterly before stalking off in the direction of the off-license, feeling crippled with hopelessness.

Now

Polly was yacking endlessly on her mobile out in the hallway. When her phone had trilled in a ringtone nearly as irritating as her voice, thirty minutes previously, Polly had been at great pains to utter in a stage whisper, that she really had to take this, it really was a very important call. She'd then shimmied her way out into the hallway like she thought she was in *Strictly Come Dancing*, or something. She really was a laughing stock.

I sat on the sofa. Polly had presented me with my lunch shortly before her mobile rang, cutting off any interaction we had been having in its tracks. She'd placed a ham sandwich, an apple and a Mars bar in front of me. She'd told me that I didn't have to come and eat it at the table if I didn't want to and that I could have it on the sofa, whilst I looked through all of Jamie's photographs. She was acting as if she was bestowing some sort of special treat upon me. I didn't seem to have an appetite anymore. It was as though I had simply stopped *being*, in many senses. Before what happened had happened, I remembered that I used to be the punchline in the office whenever lunchtime rolled around. Lunchtime always commenced at midday, and my stomach used to rumble eagerly in anticipation from quarter to twelve, onwards. I used to pat my stomach and jokingly apologise to everyone for the racket that it was making. I couldn't remember the last time my stomach had rumbled. Not in a long time anyway.

I dissected the ham sandwich in front of me. I ate a mouthful and found that it simply tasted of cardboard. Everything seemed to, these days. When I had worked at the office, I had always frequented this decadent little sandwich stop, only a stone's throw away from work. It used to serve huge doorstep style sandwiches, laden with moreish fillings like cream cheese and smoked salmon and chicken; bacon and lettuce. That had been a part of my routine for years, that sandwich shop. I used to actively look forward to lunch then; of being able to head there and try a new delicious variation, that Charlie, the sandwich shop owner would have rustled up for me. I knew that Polly was becoming really worried by my lack of eating. I saw her nibbling on her lip ferociously, anytime I turned my nose up at food that she'd brought to me, or anytime I rejected her poxy cups of tea. Polly had popped out to the sandwich shop yesterday; my old haunt. She'd excitedly brought me back five different sandwiches and an array of cakes, hoping that at least something would take my fancy. I tried; I really had tried. I'd eaten a mouthful out of each sandwich, but I couldn't bring myself to have a single bite more of any of them. They all tasted like paper, I couldn't persevere with any of them. Polly had hoped that I would at least have one cake with one of her sacred cups of tea, but they all tasted far too chocolatey and stuck to my teeth like cement. She'd burst into tears; she'd asked me if there was anything at all that she could make for me that I might actually eat. I'd made it clear that there wasn't, before picking up my bottle of wine. She'd despairingly tried to prise it from my grip, but I pushed her away. She'd run out of the room then, chuntering about how she couldn't bear to watch me mistreat myself like that. We hadn't actually spoken for the rest of the day. However, this morning, she was clearly in make-up mode, babying me as though I was a small child as opposed to a grown woman in her forties.

I could hear Polly still banging on in the hallway. I did pity the poor person on the other end of the phone. Polly really could bleat on for hours on end, even if she was getting very little to no conversational receptiveness from the other person. The woman was an egomaniac; plain and simple.

"Thanks so much, Miles," I heard her say ostentatiously.

"Thanks, we'll see you there. Oh, you know. She's the same." I heard her sigh before continuing. "That's why I don't want to put all of this on her. I just want to have it all sorted for her, so that she can turn up on Monday, knowing that a professional like yourself is going to do absolutely everything within their power to ensure that there's a conviction. Yes."

She sighed again.

"I know, I know. I'll see you there."

Polly came into the room. She looked at me sadly before trying to plaster a weak smile onto her face.

"Are you eating that up, Susanna? Come on, you must be ravenous. You hardly even touched your breakfast."

I exhaled through my nose, exasperated.

"I don't want anything," I said irritably. "I've gone off food, big time. I've only told you a million times."

I got to my feet and walked across the living room, sick of being confined to that one spot on the sofa. I walked over to the mirror and flinched back in shock at my reflection. I saw myself as gaunt, hollow, and defeated. It was as though all of the breath had been snatched from my body. If I had seen myself objectively as a different person, advancing toward me, I would have wanted to run for the hills. Except I couldn't run for the hills. I couldn't escape from this person, because she only existed as a result of this tragedy. That wasn't ever going to change. I stared hard at my reflection. *Neither was this.*

"I was talking to Miles before, Susanna," Polly said quietly.

I stared at her blankly.

"The lawyer," Polly explained.

"He's confident that we can get a conviction. There were plenty of eyewitnesses at the bar. Obviously, he can't make any guarantees but he thinks that it should go in our favour."

I turned from Polly and looked back at my reflection pensively.

"It's a sad day when a Mother is expected to be grateful that a murdering parasite is sent to jail."

Polly chewed her lip fretfully. She manoeuvred herself so that I had no other option than to face her.

"The trial will never *go* in my favour, Polly, because the trial will not bring my son back. A trial will never fill the empty void that my life has become, even one where legal 'justice' is gained."

My eyes were stinging; I knew it was a combination of upset and exhaustion.

"I am a *shell* of who I used to be, Polly. I barely eat, I look woeful and I'm plagued with thoughts that I don't want to have."

I began to cry.

"I have flashbacks, you know. I have some where Jamie's alive, some awful ones from when I saw him in the coffin. Nobody should *ever* have to see the gift that they brought into the world, being slammed into a box and left underground."

I shook, the pain was too callous and cruel today. I needed something to numb it, just slightly. I looked around the room searching for the bottle of wine I had there. Polly eyed it too. She moved for it at the same time as me, as though she was half-prepared to have a full-blown race, to get to it. I wildly leapt towards it and took a quick gulp. Polly then gently pulled the bottle from my grasp and hugged me. I was surprised by the fact that I felt momentarily secure, just for a second. Suddenly, Polly stepped back.

"Susanna, more of your hair's fallen out," Polly said gently. I knew that she was trying to remain calm but I could hear her voice crack a little.

"This is all stress, you know. I was talking to the GP about it, the other morning."

I looked at the two considerable clumps of my hair that Polly held helplessly in her hands. I was painfully aware of the bald patches that I was beginning to develop. I knew that Karen had been terribly self-conscious when some of her hair had started to fall out, a few years ago. She'd been driving herself doo-lally, panicking that there was something seriously wrong with her. Karen naturally had limp, short hair, but for years she'd had hair extensions, which meant her hair fell down past her shoulders. She'd always been delighted with her extensions until it meant that she started to resemble, a *bald eagle*, to quote her. She'd always been so wistful of my hair, which was naturally thick and shiny. She always told me that I was, a *lucky bitch*, I didn't know I was born. I felt my face crumple, thinking about how reduced I'd become. Polly misinterpreted my anguish.

"Here, here," she said quickly. She produced the paddle brush that she used on her own mane and brushed my hair, this way and that. She changed my parting, and she fluffed some of it up in a specific way. My hair looked embarrassingly greasy, but for the most part, she had managed to disguise the bald patches. I moved my head slightly. There it was again, on full display.

I could see Polly glancing down at my fingernails. I knew she was trying to be subtle, but she was far from the sole of discretion. Tactful was never exactly going to be her middle name. They'd all fallen off; as had my toenails. It was merely blood that sat on the nail beds now; I didn't have so much as a stub of a fingernail or a toenail. I felt like an alien, deformed and maddeningly different. Polly had broached this with the doctor and he didn't know why this had happened exactly, he'd never heard of that happening before. Polly had done plenty of research and was able to tell me in a tone of voice that had suggested that she thought I might be thankful for this information, was that apparently, it was actually quite common to have this happen if "you were someone, who was grieving the loss of a murdered child". From what Polly said, it seemed like quite a common ailment to experience if you were a member of the club. The club that no one wants to join.

Polly's lip wobbled.

"Susanna, please will you go and talk to someone once the trial's over? I'll come along with you, that goes without saying."

The trial.

"On Monday, I'm going to have to hear every last detail," I said thickly. "Jamie would have died *scared*. My gorgeous, happy son, the last emotion that he felt would have been fear."

Then

Polly had tried to encourage me to go back to bed when I'd plodded down to the kitchen that morning for a drink of water. She told me that I looked so tired, that she was surprised I could even stand up. She urged me to try and grab another hour or two of shut-eye. She'd bring me up some tea and toast later when I was a little more awake. I felt my hackles go up; I regarded her suspiciously. I was always tired, to coin my mum's old saying, I practically had, *shopping bags*, coming down to my chin, these days. Polly wasn't exactly used to me coming downstairs, perky and cheerful every morning, like I was about to break into some buoyant song. There was obviously some sort of reason that she wanted to keep me out of the way.

I soon found out why she was keen for me to make myself scarce. I was sitting upstairs when Polly poked her head around the door.

"Hi Susanna, I'm just nipping out to the Pharmacy to collect your prescription. I was going to do a big shop afterwards. Would you like anything?"

I shook my head. Polly looked at me, she was trying to be encouraging.

"Are you sure that you wouldn't like a wicked cake? I can't tempt you with a chocolate éclair?" she asked.

I shook my head again. Polly nodded, taking the hint.

"Okay, fair enough. I shouldn't be too long, then. Mr Jones was actually up for a walk first thing this morning, which was great. I walked him around the local streets, nowhere too far and he seemed to enjoy that. He's conked out on the sofa now though. I think he'll be dozing all day now. I think that's what you should do too…you look so pale and worn out. I do hope you're not anaemic."

She really did know how to make me feel special. I still felt suspicious as to why she was so determined to have me basing myself upstairs all day; marooned in my bedroom.

"If you do happen to hear voices downstairs, that will be Adam and his friend," she said in a low voice.

"Kayla or Kirsty, her name escapes me now. She's coming round today, I think Adam was just planning to keep her in the kitchen. So maybe it's worth letting them have some space, perhaps just giving the kitchen a wide berth until she's gone?"

I didn't reply. The doorbell rang.

"That'll be her, then," said Polly with a sigh. "Right, I'd best go downstairs and let her in. I won't be long, Susanna."

She disappeared. I heard Polly answer the door to Kayleigh, making small talk for a minute or two before taking off herself. I'd heard Polly tell Kayleigh to go on through to the kitchen, Adam was in there. He was looking forward to seeing her.

I waited until I heard the front door close shut and that I'd seen Polly's Corsa reverse out of the driveway and heading down the road, before slipping downstairs, as quiet as a mouse. Kayleigh had left the door a little ajar when she'd gone into the room, which meant that unbeknown to Adam (and Kayleigh too, I suppose), I could see and hear everything.

Kayleigh sat down at the kitchen table beside Adam. Two mugs of coffee sat down before them, as well as a small plate of biscuits. Adam looked unsettlingly like a coyote, preparing to pounce on a trusting hare. Kayleigh took his hand.

"Adam, I'm so glad that you asked me around here today. It's so great to actually see you…"

She blushed, clearly cringing.

"Obviously, the circumstances are far from great. Oh God, I feel like a right idiot."

Adam nodded; the movement was undefinably aggressive.

"I knew what you meant. Thanks for coming, I appreciate it."

Kayleigh squeezed his hand.

"No problem at all, I'm pleased to be here. I've been going out of my mind with worry, you'd been avoiding all of my calls for ages."

She tried to smile, although it was clear that she still felt undeniably hurt.

"I'm assuming you got my 4000 text messages?" she asked.

Adam tried to look apologetic, although I knew he was silently vexed. He didn't like being on the receiving end of questions, particularly when those questions were being asked by a female. I knew that he was biting back his fury, he had to concentrate on playing his part.

"Sorry, sorry, I should have got back to you. That was a bit off of me, I know. I've just had a tonne of things whirring about in my head."

Kayleigh looked at him, visibly affected.

"I'll have you know that people have always said that I'm a good listener."

Adam rolled his eyes, he picked up a biscuit and gnawed at it, crunching noisily.

"The last thing that I want to do is to heap all of my problems on you. "

Kayleigh looked at him intently, her conker-brown eyes kind and nurturing.

"You can tell me absolutely anything," she said softly. "Spill."

Adam sighed.

"It's just been awful, these last few weeks. My mum, she cannot stand to be within a ten-mile radius of me."

Kayleigh took a sip of coffee.

"She's your mum, you know that she loves the bones of you," she said softly. "She's just struggling right now. She's angry, it's normal. She'll come back to you, give her time."

Adam stared at her for a second, his expression for the most part unreadable.

"She said that she wished I had been the one who'd died, as opposed to Jamie," said Adam dryly.

Kayleigh looked visibly aghast.

"That's horrid, Adam, you shouldn't have had to hear that. But you should cut her some slack. She's all over the place, she's inevitably going to say things that she's really going to wish she could take back one day."

Kayleigh picked up a biscuit and started to nibble at it delicately. She resembled a bashful mouse, wide-eyed and wanting. It seemed so sad that she craved the attention of someone as vitriolic and menacing as Adam. She tucked a strand of her fine, fair hair behind an ear as she gazed at him expectantly. She was waiting for him to say something.

"It's not even just my mum that wonders why it couldn't have been me instead," Adam uttered finally.

"I think everybody struggles with the fact that Jamie is the one to die out of him and I. The one who was always so full of life is the one who's dead. The one who no one really gave a stuff about, is the one that's not six feet under. It doesn't make much sense, really."

Kayleigh looked at Adam with a disarming sense of longing before saying fiercely, "People *do* like you, Adam!"

Kayleigh looked at him, suddenly somewhat shy.

"I know that you are a bit of a lone ranger and you don't really mix with many people. But that doesn't mean that people don't like you, that's just your way."

She wriggled about in her seat, suddenly jumpy.

"I was chuffed when you said you were interested in me," she suddenly burst out.

"Look, you're not like Jamie and you're never going to be. You were both completely different people and that's *okay*. Personally, I actually think it would be a tad creepy if you were just some sort of clone. You don't have to pretend to be like Jamie, you don't have to pretend to be like anyone. All you have to be is yourself and that is enough."

Kayleigh was turning a little pink.

"*You're* enough, Adam. I happen to think that you're really great."

Adam didn't say a word. He sat there, non-committal. He wanted her to nervously burble until she'd laid down every single card of hers on the table, and he could sit there, smug and satisfied in the knowledge that she evidently felt on edge around him. She had to placate him by being motor mouth all of the time, divulging her innermost thoughts and feelings, whilst he didn't share anything.

"I want you to know that I want to be there for you, throughout the trial and everything," Kayleigh said, with solemn intensity. "I know how difficult it will be for your family. I thought it was bad enough, losing my dad two years back, but that was so different. It was of natural causes for a start, it wasn't *murder*. We didn't have to go through a trial, nothing like that. This…it's in a totally different league of its own."

She chewed her lip, looking emotional.

"I can't imagine how terrible things must feel just now, Adam. I know you must feel so lonely and have so much to say. I know I've always found it tough talking to my family about how I feel. You can always talk to me though, use me as a sounding board, get everything off your chest."

Adam feigned looking reticent.

"If I told you something, would you promise that it would stay between us?" he asked, masquerading as a human being in possession with a heart.

Kayleigh nodded; her neck practically clicked because she nodded so hard. Her eyes bulged out, and she looked alarmingly like a scared small child, trying to evade getting into trouble.

"Mum's the word," she replied seriously.

Adam stretched, enjoying Kayleigh's undivided attention.

"Jamie and I hadn't actually been on the best of terms, on the night that he was killed," he said cryptically.

"We'd had words, it's gutting really. We were always so tight-knit as brothers but it just seems so unfair that the one time where we butted heads, had to happen on the same night that he was stabbed to death."

He pretended to look as though he was near tears.

"I had been a grade A wally, testing everyone's patience, being a right prat. I hate myself now though, if only I hadn't of been such a berk, I wouldn't be fretting all of the time now, wondering if Jamie died hating me."

Kayleigh hugged him, swift and sensitive.

"All families fight, Adam," she said firmly.

"I have three sisters and to be honest, we usually do nothing *but* fight. We're always getting on each other's nerves, but we know at the end of the day, how much we all mean to one another. Jamie knew that you just idolised him and I'm sure that he wouldn't have been without you for the world."

Adam sniffed; he was trying to appear at a low ebb.

"I do hate the fact that I'll never really know," he said. "Jamie's dead now and I'm never going to be able to right any wrongs that I made in the past. It just makes me feel like crap, really."

He squeezed out a crocodile tear.

"I'm just so alone, Kayleigh," he snivelled sadistically.

She pulled him close to her, she hugged him tightly for a couple of minutes. He didn't make any effort to hug her back. The tighter that she hugged him, the more resistant he became to reciprocating in any way.

"You've always got me," she vowed as he pulled away from her completely.

"Promise?" he pressed.

"I promise," she said as she held his hand. With her other hand, Kayleigh reached out to take another biscuit from the plate.

Kayleigh was one of those bird-like females, with matchstick arms and legs. Adam looked at her as though she was disgusting.

"Maybe, leave off the biscuits, eh?" he said acidly, as he looked critically at her flat stomach. "You don't want to pile on the pounds, do you?"

Kayleigh dropped the biscuit as though it was boiling hot. She peered down at her own stomach disapprovingly.

Adam rammed three biscuits into his mouth at once. I could see properly which biscuits they were now. Of course, Jammy Dodgers. His favourites.

"I always call these Jamie Dodgers," he said with his mouth full. "It always makes me feel a bit closer to him," he said, with the crumbs spraying revoltingly.

Kayleigh peered at him fearfully, desperate to know what the right thing to say was. I felt debilitated with disgust, looking at him.

Now

I sat on the living room floor, Mr Jones' head on my lap. This seemed rather fitting, as I was leafing through all of Jamie's photographs and I stumbled across the first photo that was ever taken of Jamie with Mr Jones. Dean had taken the photo; I could remember that. Jamie's beam was a mile-wide, he'd always pined for a puppy and here he finally was, with his canine companion. He was overjoyed, he'd instantly picked Mr Jones up upon his arrival and hugged him close to his chest, kissing the top of his velvety head. Dean had suggested that I got into the photo too. Jamie, Mr Jones and I. I'd still been in my pyjamas, my hair tied back in a topknot. I'd laughed, I'd made it clear that he had no chance of getting me in a photograph, looking like that. Jamie had pleaded with me to come and get my photo taken too, but I had insisted that the camera would probably break if it was to capture me looking such a mess. I badly wished I'd gone into the photo now, why did I care that I was in my old pyjamas with my hair all scraped back? Why couldn't I have just seen that the most important thing about that photograph would have been that I was standing there with my perfect little boy and his gorgeous puppy? I felt so *infuriated* with myself.

I showed the photograph to Mr Jones, irrationally hoping that he'd recognise a younger self and a younger Jamie, that he'd somehow react to it. Mr Jones didn't so much as glance at the photograph, he just gazed up at me attentively, with his adoring, compassionate eyes. Mr Jones was a dear old dog. I stroked him gently, wondering if there were any more photos with Mr Jones. Considering how close Jamie had been to Mr Jones, there weren't as many photos, as I would have thought there would have been. There were funny ones of course. I discovered a small sheaf of photos that had hilariously captured Mr Jones and Jamie dozing on the sofa, heads both comically lolling, in a near-identical fashion. I found a photograph of Jamie from a couple of years back dressed up as Batman, Mr Jones clad in a Robin costume that Jamie had managed to source for him on the Internet. They both looked adorable, it had been on the slideshow that I'd made of photographs for Jamie's 21st. Everyone had cooed, Mr Jones, who of course was in attendance at the party, even got a special shout-out and round of applause at the end. It had been a photo that I had always intended to get framed. I didn't know why I hadn't, why had I never gone into town, picked up a really nice frame, stuck the photo in and displayed it with pride on the mantelpiece? Why did I constantly put off doing things, what on earth was I wasting the time on instead?

I was tempted to pick up the bottle of wine which was by my side, but there was something about Mr Jones' level stare, that stopped me. I tickled him behind his ears. He started to stretch out, snuggling his head down into his paws. It looked as though the walk down memory lane had exhausted him; he needed to grab forty winks. Polly came into the room, holding an ever-present cup of tea. She resembled Kermit the frog in a green towelling dressing gown. I knew she was doing her level best to contain a yawn, but it was clear that she was tired.

"Aww, look at Mr Jones," she said affectionately. He was snoring softly now, in the land of nod.

"I know how he feels. I don't know about you, Susanna, but I'm absolutely shattered."

I ignored her. I knew what she was going to suggest, but I didn't want to leave the photos for the evening; I wanted to stay up and remember Jamie. To have all of these good memories at the epicentre of my mind. As after all, I was aware that I was going to hear information tomorrow, that had the capacity to ruin all of the good memories that I actually had of Jamie. I felt engulfed by fear at the thought of the details I was going to hear tomorrow, etching their way permanently into my mind so that they occupied my every waking thought, irreversibly decaying and infecting all of my thoughts about Jamie's life.

"Everyone has a happy ending," I remembered that was what Tom had said to me once, shortly before he died.

"I've had a short life, yes, I'd be the first to say that. But I've met you, my dream wife and I have a wonderful family and amazing friends. I've left a legacy in James and he is going to grow up to be magnificent. I can feel it in my bones."

I remembered him saying with a reflective sigh, "I can honestly say that I'm happy at the end, Suze. So, don't ever think of all this as anything but. Your living happy ending is James."

I felt myself fighting back tears. Tom's words had been even more profound than what he had realised, my living happy ending really had been Jamie. So, if he wasn't living anymore, where did that leave me exactly? Plus, Jamie's ending had been far from happy. I'd seen his body; I'd seen the extent of the injuries inflicted upon him. That had been as far from a happy ending as what you could get, but it had still been his ending. His sunny existence ended just like that. It was just so catastrophic.

I felt a tear starting to slide down my face. Polly stroked my hair, as though I was a little girl.

"Susanna, you poor love, you're worn out."

She looked at me worriedly.

"Do you think it might be an idea to grab an early night?" she suggested tentatively.

"It's a really long day that we've got ahead of us tomorrow."

I didn't look at her. I stayed looking at Jamie's photographs. I knew it was ridiculous, but I couldn't help but will him to step out of his photographs, to be here, to be alive again.

"Come on," I murmured to his smiling face pleadingly.

Polly misunderstood, she thought that I was talking to her.

"I'll help you up to bed, Susanna. Tomorrow's going to be really heavy going. It's going to take its toll on all of us massively. You really need to try and get as much sleep as possible."

I turned on her, snapping fiercely.

"I don't sleep, you know that, for crying out loud! To sleep, I'd have to possess the ability to unwind, relax. Something that I'm incapable of doing these days."

Polly looked as though she was trying hard to not lose her temper. She ran a hand through her hair, looking troubled.

"Why don't you go up and change into your pyjamas, Susanna? Then, you can come back down, look through your photographs and I'll make you a nice camomile tea, that should hopefully help you to grab a few decent hours of kip, at the very least."

It seemed like too much effort to argue with her. I rose to my feet, feeling like an old woman as I edged my way up the stairs. My staircase wasn't particularly big, but it felt as though I was making a gruelling journey, as though I was scaling Everest or something. I felt disconcerted by the knowledge that my elderly mother could have probably bounded up those stairs, in comparison to me. I felt so ancient, so inept. It was awful.

I shuffled across the landing silently, heading in the direction of my room. I had to pass Adam's bedroom on the way. His door was slightly ajar and I could hear him talking to someone, in a low, insistent voice. I hovered outside of his door, wanting to listen in.

"I wish I could take all of this upset away from you," said Kayleigh, who appeared to practically be in tears.

"I can't even imagine how you must be feeling right now, with what lies ahead. I just want you to know that I'll be at the Court tomorrow, on your team, every step of the way. I'm in this for the long haul, Adam."

It seemed that it was a FaceTime call, as opposed to a regular phone call.

"There's something that you could do," he said, his tone suggesting and sinister.

"Anything," Kayleigh replied placatingly, her eyes like saucers.

"It's so hard at the moment," Adam said, feigning tears.

"All I can think about is the trial, about Jamie. But it's not good for me to constantly be focusing on that, it's only natural that I'm going to need a distraction every once in a while. So, that's where you come in."

Kayleigh stared at him, intent and pandering. She looked alarmingly like someone awaiting an order.

"Send me some pics," he uttered, with an undeniable threatening undertone.

Kayleigh looked confused.

"What, of myself? God, I'm in my ratty old hoodie at the moment, I don't think you want a photo like that on your phone."

Adam smirked.

"Lose the hoodie, Kayleigh. Lose everything. I want to see *you*, completely stripped back, not hiding behind any clothes."

Kayleigh looked uncomfortable.

"I don't know," she said anxiously, staring down at her lap. "I've never done anything like that before; no one's ever asked me to send those sorts of photos."

Adam smirked.

"Nobody has ever given you a second look before me. All the other guys at school are generic, they ask the fit girls. You know, girls like Alexa, girls like Gemma. The ones that get the blood racing, the ones that most guys would give their right arm to see photos like that of, standing there, legs spread in just a pair of heels."

He paused, surveying her hesitancy.

"They're the *sexy* girls Kayleigh, you're never going to be the kind of girl that's going to get male attention, you're never going to make most guys' engines rev. But *I've* seen something in you, some potential, you could say. I think you *could* be fit if you put the effort in. This is what girls do now Kayleigh, it's part of a 21st-century relationship. All the Darcy and Elizabeth style romances, they're not real. This is how it works these days."

Kayleigh looked on the verge of tears. She looked alarmingly *young*.

"You won't show them to anyone, will you Adam?" she asked desperately. "I would rather die than have photos like that doing the rounds."

"I don't talk to anyone at school," he slimed, spiteful and smirking. "Who would I really show? No, they will be for my eyes and my eyes only."

Kayleigh looked as though she'd struck gold all of a sudden like she had found a solution.

"I could come around," she suggested.

"I could be with you in the flesh, you wouldn't have to have the photos…"

"No," he interjected abruptly, appearing somewhat repulsed at the suggestion of actually physically doing anything with her.

"Stick with the photos. And no chickening out, no underwear, no anything. And send a video too. That would be good."

I walked to my room. What I had just witnessed was horrifying, I knew that, but I was too tired to think about it properly, to give it any brain space. I saw that Polly had put fresh bed sheets on my bed. She appeared to have bought me a new pair of pyjamas too, that sat neatly folded in a lavender pile, on my pillow. I put them on, although they weren't my taste at all. I felt like a walking Pomo violet.

I edged my way along the landing again. I could hear Adam say, "Good girl," over and over again. I felt sickened. His hand was down his trousers.

I hurried downstairs to find that Polly had left a cup of camomile tea, sitting for me in the living room.

"Drink that up, Susanna, before it gets cold," Polly said suddenly, as she came into the living room from the kitchen, munching biscuits. Jammy Dodgers. I hated those things. She offered me one, but I refused.

Adam suddenly came into the living room. Polly glanced at him, concerned.

"You okay, lovie? I thought you'd decided to call it a night, ages ago."

Adam sighed.

"Couldn't sleep. Not that I was expecting to. I think I always knew that tonight was going to be a sleepless night."

He looked down at the floor at all of the photographs spread out of Jamie.

"I'm scared about tomorrow," he said quietly. "I'm scared about how it's all going to pan out."

He sniffed slightly.

"I just miss J so much."

He put his hand on my shoulder. I felt too exhausted to resist.

The Next Day

I walked into the Court Room the next day, Polly on one side, Adam on the other. I felt completely drained and the day had barely begun. It wasn't even 9 am and I already felt as though today had gone on for a lifetime.

The day had already been a disaster. Polly had said yesterday evening that she was a little bit concerned about where she was going to park for the Court tomorrow. She said the last thing that she wanted was for us to end up arriving there late. She conceded that it would be best for us to get a taxi to the Court and back home when it was over. She imparted this information to me, in a way that would suggest I'd punch the air and cheer, like it was some sort of special treat travelling to the Court the next day for the trial taking place, because of my murdered child. She really was an imbecile.

The taxi had arrived to pick us up at ten to eight. Polly had done nothing but flap and fuss, the whole time we were in the taxi. She'd ordered herself a new handbag for the day, she's justified it by saying that all of her handbags were colourful that would look wholly inappropriate at a murder trial. She needed a nice, smart handbag, a glossy matte-black colour. She had insisted that I could borrow it anytime I fancied after the trial because it really was a great little bag, a really nice size and a great make.

"I know it was really naughty buying myself a Coach handbag when it wasn't my birthday or Christmas or anything, but I wanted to do our Jamie proud. Plus, I like to think that he'd be pleased that I was treating myself. Life's too short, after all."

I'd regarded her warily as she'd spouted all of this drivel, wondering if she was genuinely cretinous or callous.

Polly wriggled uncomfortably, for the duration of our journey. I'd assumed that she was merely nervous, but she soon announced to everyone that she just couldn't seem to sit comfortably, for love nor money, her skirt was digging in ever so painfully.

"I knew I should have gone a size up in this pencil skirt, they're unforgiving," she chuntered to herself. "I should have worn something with an elasticated waist. Jesus, I'll have no circulation by 11 am at this rate. It's all those bloody biscuits, I'm telling you. I'm telling you, after today, I'm never touching a Jammy Dodger again, they're my downfall."

Adam nodded at her politely. I couldn't bear to acknowledge either of them. I stared stonily out of the window, trying to freeze the pair of them out. Polly, being the prima-donna that she was, then insisted that the taxi took a pit stop outside a coffee shop. She said that she couldn't speak for anyone else, but that she herself was *parched*, she needed to have a flat white before she fainted. Polly wobbled out of the car, her backside waggling ludicrously as she made her way into the coffee shop. Adam glanced over in my direction; it was as though he was deliberating whether to instigate a conversation with me. I couldn't think of anything worse. The taxi driver clearly found the silence maddening, he started jabbering on about the weather. He prattled on about how grey the sky was; it would be tipping it down by midday, watch this space. It was all so mind numbing. I didn't so much as bother to grunt in reply. He soon gave up.

Polly reappeared again; laden with a little plastic holder, containing takeaway drinks. She drank her own coffee in seconds, and she started making a strange half-coughing sound, as though she was trying to cope with the burning sensation in her throat, that had happened as a direct consequence of pouring scalding coffee down her. I didn't take a single sip out of the latte that she had got for me. Adam on the other hand guzzled his cappuccino so eagerly that he ended up spilling some of it, he wound up with coffee dribbling down his tie. He swore under his breath, as he furiously rubbed at it, but this just served in making the stain even worse. Polly daubed and dabbed at him, in full-blown doting Aunt mode, all for the taxi driver's benefit. She even gave him the come-hither eyes, when she thanked him ostentatiously, as we clambered out of the taxi, outside the Court. On the day of the trial. When I thought it was impossible for her to disgust me anymore, she somehow managed to.

I wished that I could just walk into the Courtroom alone. I sure as hell emotionally was, so I failed to see why I couldn't just do this for real. Adam attempted to take my hand but I couldn't bear to have him near me. I wedged both of my hands into my blazer pockets pointedly, to make it clear that I didn't want him near me. I looked at the people sitting in the Public Gallery. Kayleigh was there, strands of her pale hair pinned back severely in a sterile updo. She looked so young sitting there in her smart black jacket and fitted trousers, like a young girl dressing up in her mum's clothes. She sat, hunched and anticipating in her seat. She looked as though she was questioning as to why on earth she'd even come here. Adam stared right through her, as though he had never set eyes on her in his life. Kayleigh looked defeated, she shrunk down even further.

Max was sitting on the other side of Kayleigh, holding an inconsolable Rachel. The trial hadn't even started, but Rachel was already bawling into Max's chest. She'd clearly tried to make an effort, her hair was newly washed, she wore a pencil-grey work dress. Her shoulders shook uncontrollably, as she sobbed into Max. Her face, for the most part, was hidden, but Max's wasn't. I could see the tenderness on his face; the desire to protect her from anything and everything that could cause her harm. He whispered soothingly into her head and she looked up at him, her eyes tear-filled as she listened to him earnestly, something that I couldn't quite catch. I didn't look at them and see two grieving friends, comforting each other. I saw *that* when I looked further along the row and saw lots of Jamie's other friends, sitting there stiffly in their Sunday best, red-eyed and tense. This was different, Max and Rachel's dynamic was different. There was something unshakeably intimate about the way with which they looked at each other, the tenderness between them. I noticed that Tilly was sitting on Rachel's other side, as though they were suddenly joined at the hip. Tilly's hair was tied back at the nape of her neck in a low bun, her make-up was heavy and there was uncharacteristic steel, with her demeanour that I'd never seen before in her. I'd known her since she was a babe in arms and I had never seen her look powerful, confident. She did today.

Karen and Geoff were there too. Geoff had turned a startling shade of beetroot, clearly, the tension was starting to get under his skin, one way or another. Karen sat as stiff as an ironing board, looking like she would rather be anywhere else. I frowned, as I regarded a noticeable ladder in her tights. I couldn't help but glower. Karen noticed my disapproval and looked down critically at herself. She spotted the ladder on her tights and cringed inwardly. All she had to do today, was dress appropriately. She hadn't even been able to do that.

Dave and Kev had also attended too, which I was relatively surprised at. I knew that they'd mentioned that they'd like to come, but I had wondered if that was simply waffle. Polly had told me this morning as she tried to wheedle with me to eat up the egg and toast that she'd made me that they were shutting up the garage today as a mark of respect to Jamie. They had done this the day after he'd been murdered, the day of his funeral too. I supposed it was quite sweet of them, really. I noticed their punchiness as they sat there; it was as if Dave in particular was gearing up for a fight. I followed Dave's eye line to see what was incensing him so much. I looked over at the people sitting there, that I didn't know. It was obvious as to who they were there for. They were the killer's family.

I stared directly at the Mother, who was clad in a trouser suit, her hair yanked back in a spiky ponytail. I blotted out everyone else she was sitting with, I only looked at her. Her face was long and pinched, she appeared to have a tonne of concealer on, but no amount of make-up could hide the bags under her eyes. She looked back arrogantly in my direction as though she was suddenly aware of the scrutiny. I could tell that she was trying to, but despite her best efforts, she never quite seemed to be able to look me in the eye.

Then the words of the Bailiff boomed across the Courtroom.

"All rise. The Court of London Magistrates is now in session. The Honourable Judge McAvoy presiding."

Along with everyone else, I staggered to my feet, my legs wobbling slightly. I willed them not to wobble, especially as I was painfully aware that all eyes from the killer's family were on me. A female judge, around my age, entered and slowly took her seat.

I think that massive misconceptions exist about justice and what it means, exactly. You are led to believe that you will obtain closure, peace and contentment from a trial. It is the end of a horrific chapter that's what the insinuation always is, that it will provide a line under everything. However, the difficult truth is that Jamie is the only source that can provide me with closure. Yet, he is heartbreakingly unobtainable. A state of unrest, of incompleteness, is unfortunately all I will know, from here on out.

My thoughts are interrupted by the chilling words, "Bring out the defendant, Travis Joshua Smith."

I saw a young, revolting man emerge. His chin jutted upwards cockily. He was small and scrawny, his hair coal-black and greasy. You would have thought that he largely would have been a nondescript figure. But there was a poison that penetrated from him, a bestiality. He emitted crass remorselessness. He appeared so unrelenting and so unapologetic, that it was physically repugnant to witness.

“I love you, son. You’ve got this,” his Mother mouthed down, from the public gallery. She had the unsettling demeanour of a Mother cheering on her son for the big win at a sports match.

I found myself shaking with distress. I’d thought about what it would be like to see him, of course, I had. I knew it would be unbearably difficult but I thought that due to this, I’d barely be able to look at the murderer straight on. But, surprisingly, I was unable to tear my eyes away from the killer that had caused my boy’s life to end as well as my world. Of course, I wanted to tear my gaze away, because he sickened me to the core. But I seemed physically unable to do that. I noted everything, the boyish haircut which was clearly an evident attempt to make him look younger and therefore more innocent than what he was. I noted the shifty stance, the black shoes on his feet that were clearly a half-size too big for him. I felt sick because I recognised the shoes. Adam had the same pair. I resisted the urge to convulse, but I made a mental note to burn the shoes, the minute I returned home. I looked at his face. I think it would have been naïve to expect someone that could inflict such casual cruelty to ever feel sorry. Someone that stabbed someone thirty-two times, even after the victim was dead, after having attempted to sexually assault someone, will never be sorry. Unsurprisingly, there isn’t even the faintest glimmer of shame, the tiniest shred of remorse during his cross-examination. If anything, he looked bored.

“Cocky little bastard – what I would give to punch that smirk off that ugly mug of his,” I heard Dave growl from behind me.

Travis sucked his teeth the whole time and shifted about as if he couldn’t even be bothered to be there.

The words he uttered, interrupted my train of thought. He looked right up at me, craning his neck right back to make level eye contact.

“I didn’t do anything,” he said hatefully.

He didn’t face up to what he’d done. He didn’t face up to what he *was*.

The details start to come then, heinous and abominable. The people around me started to cry; Polly weeping steadily at my side.

The words, “A nerve in his spine was broken. He didn’t stand a chance,” appeared to echo.

Adam sobbed hard, his shoulders shaking.

I suppose, for a long time, a part of me had always pitied Adam. Naturally introverted and a *loner*, I think he’d always struggled being in Jamie’s shadow. Jamie was always going to be a hard act to follow and particularly for someone as dark and grisly as Adam. There was always an element of odiousness to Adam's character that I could never quite define properly. I suppose it was resentment, bitterness probably, at always being second best. I watched Adam, weeping and wailing and felt nothing. I think it was because I knew that he'd privately be revelling that strong, adored Jamie was the vulnerable one for once, ultimately paying the price for his courageous nature, an aspect of Jamie's personality that I'd known he'd always envied vitriolically.

The trial proceeded. I could hear unrelenting sound, white noise for the most part, squirming and worming into every single tiny squiggle of my brain.

I then heard the words:

"We will now hear the Victim Impact statement, written by James Wright's family."

The Next Week

I sat there in the public gallery; hollowed and withered. The words of Judge McAvoy startled me into sitting up straighter, lifting my head and tearing my gaze away from my shoes.

"Foreman, please stand."

I glanced over at the young man in his mid-twenties. He was trying to appear composed, but when I looked at him closely, I could see that he was shaking slightly.

"Have you reached a verdict upon which ten of you agree?" enquired Judge McAvoy; her tone crisp and clipped.

The Foreman nodded before confirming, "Yes."

I could feel an audible intake of breath from those around me.

"Do you find the defendant guilty of murdering James Michael Wright?" demanded Judge McAvoy.

The atmosphere in the Courtroom was eerie; it felt spookily silent, to such an extreme extent that I was fairly sure that it would have been possible to hear a pin drop.

"Yes," the Foreman stated suddenly.

Dave and Kev whooped loudly.

"Enjoy prison with the big boys, you sick little fucker!" shouted Dave.

Jamie's friends hugged each other, undeniably delighted. I looked at Polly. She squeezed my hand tightly before turning around to face Karen and Geoff. She was elated that was plain to see. They both squeezed her on the shoulder, before saying "Well done" to her, as though she had personally done something to secure the verdict. This struck me as such a stupid thing to say.

I looked around in disbelief, at all of the different reactions. Tilly looked visibly relieved, she closed her eyes and breathed out, as though she had finally been given pain relief after an encumbering ailment. Rachel was hysterical, she buried her head in Max's shoulder muttering to him. He kissed the top of her head blatantly, seemingly unbothered as to whether I noticed it or not.

"He's been done proud, Rach," he said with a tearful sense of tenacity.

"That low-life has been punished. Justice has been served."

I noticed that Adam had turned around to Kayleigh, he smiled at her creepily. She looked nervous, but she leaned forward to hug him. He made a point of brushing her chest with his wiry fingers, before hissing at her threateningly, "Later."

Kayleigh looked as though the weight of the world had descended upon her shoulders.

Travis' mother meanwhile was screaming. She practically threw herself from the public galley when Judge McAvoy sentenced him to ten years in prison. Travis himself looked completely galled, as though he was actually speechless, for once in his life.

"It's okay, babe, it's okay!" his mother called down to him hysterically.

"We'll get an appeal! Stay strong babe, keep your chin up! I'll come and visit you, as soon as I can, babe!"

She sobbed hopelessly in the arms of her family, claiming that it was an outrage, she'd never stop fighting for him, not whilst there was still breath in her body.

"I've lost my boy," she wept into the shoulder of her husband.

"I've lost my baby."

I stared at her steadily. She didn't look in my direction, but her unease was clear. They lagged behind in the Courtroom as we left, clearly wanting to avoid being around myself and Jamie's loved ones in the communal areas.

I looked around at the sights before me, everyone was rejoicing. I wondered if they'd all received different news, a different verdict. Polly practically started a conga, she was hurtling round, hugging everyone tightly and talking about how great, great, great it all was. She practically cheered when Miles, the lawyer appeared. Polly wound her arms around his neck, giving him a huge hug as she expressed that to her personally, he was an amazing barrister, a real credit to the law profession. Polly insisted upon Miles taking a bow as everyone cheered and clapped. I assumed that he would refuse, but he didn't. He actually did bow, as though he had just been performing on the stage.

It then seemed to dawn on Polly that she had not yet spoken to me. She came rushing up to me; she snaked an arm around my waist.

"Oh Susanna, this is *good* news. I think we should all go back and celebrate, that killer can't roam the streets. He's been locked up for a decade. Come on, we'll all go back to the house and we can have some tea. I think it would be nice to reminisce about Jamie, to think about him, to remember him. What do you think? Does that sound like a plan?"

I could barely bring myself to look at her; to look at any of them.

"I'm going on a walk," I said abruptly as I tore myself away from Polly. I made for the exit, with everyone peering uncertainly after me.

The Long Road Ahead

I felt as though I'd been spat out of the Courtroom back into the real world again; it was throwing and disarming. I registered the busy people racing by with their busy lives, everything non-stop, everything purposeful. I used to be like them once. Back before I joined the club that no one ever wishes to become a member of.

I set off down the road, knowing where I was going. It was the only place I could go to, on a day like today.

Ten years. In the eyes of the law, that is a great result. But what's ten years to a lifetime of heartache, to a lifetime of grief and loss? That murderer is going to be fed and watered, he'll be allowed Countdown in the evenings, and visits from his mother. He'll be freed after probably serving half of his sentencing and he'll be loose on the streets again. Jamie isn't going to live again.

I turned the corner, passing a pub. I eyed it wistfully, but I resisted temptation and walked on, away from it.

Jamie's loss is still indescribably raw, with a potency that is hard to define. He was honourable. Respectable. Gorgeous. In fact, he almost had to be as funny as he was in order to remain approachable. Which he was. Everyone loved him. Memories of Jamie from babyhood to adulthood swirled around my head like hyperactive butterflies, there were so many memories being experienced in quick succession, that it felt as though my head was pulsing. I heard his laugh; jovial and comforting.

That was the thing about Jamie, he was *one of the good guys*. He fought for the vulnerable; the beaten-down and he challenged vindictiveness head-on, yet with his usual gentlemanly approach. People gravitated toward him because of his vibrancy, his energy just had a positive effect on anyone he encountered. The world badly needs more Jamie's. Today of all days has taught me that the world is in desperate need of good.

I missed Jamie so much that it hurt. There was only one place now, where I felt remotely close to him. I turned around the next corner, quickening my pace. I was getting closer; I was practically there.

I started the long walk up to the graveyard. That killer's mother can sit across from him at a table. I have to talk to the ground, to look at a headstone that I feel personally never quite did Jamie justice. *Beloved son*, will never quite cut it, he was and always will be my life.

I made my way towards his grave, taking care because the path was so uneven, so laden with cracks. That was supposed to be unlucky, wasn't it? Oh, well, my luck ran out a long time ago.

I could see Jamie's grave. There were mountains of flowers by it, bright and cheerful. It looked as though there were some notes too, but I felt no inclination to read any of them. It appeared that quite a few people had been here this morning to visit his grave, to leave their flowers, to think about him today as the trial concluded. The trial has concluded. My grief hasn't. Grief is an insidiously isolating experience. The *friends* have inevitably disappeared. They bob around to be seen on days like this, but they've become tired of strained small talk, and awkward silences. I looked at Jamie's grave, now I was up closer, I really could see that it was heaving with flowers. I suppose that has become the role of the friends; they don't persevere with me, but they do ensure that Jamie's grave is constantly adorned with fresh flowers. Although, of course, there will be a time when they'll stop doing that too. When they'll simply let the flowers wilt. Like the way they've left me to.

I sat down on the grass, by Jamie's grave. I stroked his headstone.

"Hey, J," I said softly to him.

So, how do I fill the great empty expanse of my days, you may wonder? I wake and for a few moments, I'll forget. I'll be thinking of all the different things that I need to do that day. How I'll nip into the office early so that I can leave at four. Then that gives me plenty of time to get home in time to make a nice family meal, to have a good catch-up with Jamie. *Jamie.* Then it will descend on me, the grief, the angst, the *agony.* So, in a bid to get a respite from it, I drink excessively.

I pulled my hip flask out of my clutch bag. I never went anywhere without it, these days.

I drink excessively now, in a bid to blot the pain out. Although then, of course, it will come back with a vengeance; destructive and debilitating. So, I'll drink again. And the cycle will continue.

Was justice served today? I slurped from the hip flask; feeling myself sinking as I crouched down, my face next to Jamie's headstone. No, it most certainly wasn't. Atonement perhaps, that's the most that could be said for what happened today. If there was justice, I would be seeing Jamie alive and well at home, as opposed to dead and buried at the graveyard.

Memories of Jamie from babyhood to adulthood ricocheted through my mind. His cry as a baby, his laugh as an adult. Judge McAvoy's voice interrupted me. "Travis Joshua Smith, you have been found guilty of the murder of James Michael Wright. You will be sentenced to ten years in prison."

I cried hard, the memories pounded through my mind, head, throbbingly debilitating. I was trying to fight the memory of seeing Jamie dead, of seeing what that murderer had taken from me.

I heard Judge McAvoy's voice again. "Susanna Hilary Wright, your son James Michael Wright was murdered. You are condemned to a life sentence."